Big Momma Didn't Tell Me **This** Would Happen!
And
Violence Should NOT Be Your Family Legacy!

This book is a work of fiction. The names, characters, place and incidents are either the products of the author's imagination or used fictitiously. Any resemblance to actual persons, living or dead, events or locales is entirely coincidental.

Copyright © 2015 by Darlene Greene
All rights reserved
ISBN 9781511591195
9781329378179

"HOW DOES HE LOVE ME, LET ME COUNT THE WAYS"

1. HE CONTROLS MY EVERY MOVE - *He likes to look out for me.*
2. I CANNOT DO ANYTHING OR GO ANYPLACE WITHOUT HIS PERMISSION - *He protects me so nothing bad will happen to me.*
3. HE REMINDS ME WHAT A LOSER I AM AND WITHOUT HIM I WOULD BE ALONE - *I need to remember that I am lucky to have him.*
4. HE THREATENS TO KILL ME OR MY CHILDREN WHEN I STAND UP TO HIM - *Because my place is with him and he knows best.*
5. HE TAKES ALL OF MY MONEY (I DON'T NEED MONEY I HAVE HIM) - *He is so generous!*
6. HE WOULD NOT HIT ME IF I DON'T PROVOKE HIM - *I have to learn to appreciate him.*
7. WHEN HE BROKE MY ARM, HE MADE DINNER - *He is very thoughtful.*
8. HE DRIVES ME EVERYPLACE I GO -- EVEN TO WORK - *He knows I work hard; this saves me the trouble of driving myself.*
9. HE SCREENS MY CALLS SO I AM NOT BOTHERED BY FRIENDS AND FAMILY - *I need my rest.*
10. HE THINKS I LOOK FINE NATURALLY, SO THERE IS NO NEED TO HAVE MY HAIR DONE OR WEAR MAKEUP - *I am beautiful on the inside.*
11. I CAN'T DO ANYTHING RIGHT; I AM LUCKY TO HAVE HIM - *Where would I be without him?*
12. IF I WOULD ONLY LISTEN HE WOULDN'T NEED TO HIT ME -- AFTER ALL HE DOES IT FOR MY OWN GOOD - **When will I learn?**

Ina Mae Greene Foundation - For My Sisters

DEDICATION

*To my friend, gone but never forgotten.
You will be missed, and always,*

For My Sisters

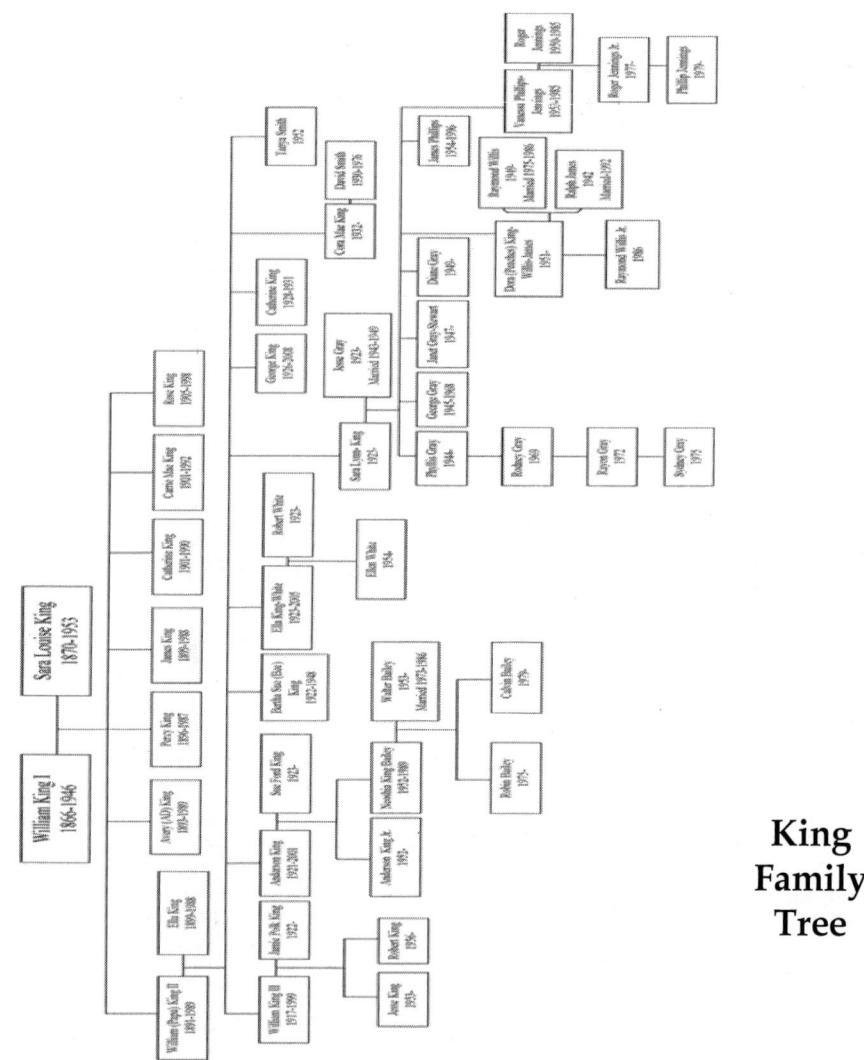

King Family Tree

Table of Contents

TITLE PAGE/COPYRIGHT	
"HOW DOES HE LOVE ME,	2
LET ME COUNT THE WAYS"	2
DEDICATION	3
KING FAMILY TREE	4
ACKNOWLEDGMENTS	7
PROLOGUE	7
CHAPTER 1	11
"NEVER GONNNA GIVE YOU UP"	19
"WHEN LIFE GIVES YOU LEMONS"	34
"EVERY BODY WANTS TO RULE THE WORLD"	42
"IN MY NEXT LIFE I HOPE I AM NOT A GIRL"	52
"WE ARE FAMILY-I'VE GOT ALL MY SISTERS WITH ME"	72
"IT TAKES A FOOL TO LEARN THAT	90
MY MOTHER- SARA LYNN KING-GRAY--PHILLIP'S-CHILDREN	103
"WHAT BECOMES OF A BROKEN HEARTED?"	118
"A TIME TO LAUGH A TIME TO CRY"	130
"SOMEDAY, CHANGE IS GONNA COME"	134
"NOWHERE TO RUN—NOWHERE TO HIDE"	147
"LIVE LAUGH LOVE"	156
"I WANT TO BE YOUR LAST LOVE"	174
READERS' POLL	177

ALTERNATIVE ENDING	179
"WILL YOU STILL LOVE ME TOMORROW"?!	180
AFTERWORD	187
WHERE TO GO FOR HELP	190
RED FLAGS AND WARNING SIGNS	193
RED FLAGS	195
LEGAL HELP, CHILD CUSTODY	197
AND DIVORCE	197
HOW TO HELP A FRIEND WHO IS IN AN ABUSIVE RELATIONSHIP	198
MY CHECK LIST FOR LOVING ME FIRST	200
RESOURCE LIST	201
SAFETY PLAN	207
WORKBOOK	207
REFERENCES	212
AUTHOR'S NOTES	213
ABOUT THE AUTHOR	215

ACKNOWLEDGMENTS

I want to thank the elder women in my family who taught me so much about being a complete person.
Growing up around my great-aunts — (my grandfather's sisters), who were my teachers early in life; before I knew there were lessons to learn.

I'd sit and listen in on the talks they had over coffee at the kitchen table on Saturday mornings. *Oh the stories they would tell*, they introduced me to a world of laughter and wonder! For those lessons I will be eternally grateful. Thank You! I thank my husband, who is my friend and my partner. He taught me what real love is and how to be in a relationship without sacrificing who I was to be "his woman"! Thank You!

I thank my children for accepting that I wanted to change the world and jumping in to help me win the fight and never complained when I was busy and away from home trying to help other families find peace and safety, thank you!

To other victim's advocates who have been in the trenches working hard everyday to save the lives of women and children across the country, without adequate compensation or recognition, yet you pushed forward. Without you there would be no movement to stop this crime, thank you.

To my siblings who have allowed me to tell the story of our family secrets and tragedies over and over so that we can try and spare another family the pain and loss that we all have suffered! Thank You!

And to my sister friends who were my helpers raising my children, giving me advice, crying with me when it seemed that I couldn't go on, thank you, and for being my support in tough times.

Thank you

PROLOGUE

⌘

MADISONVILLE MISSISSIPPI 2013

I grew up in a family of strong women, strong in every situation unless it involved men. For some reason women, even strong women fall apart when it comes to a man.
We lose our good and common sense, and make decisions that we cannot explain when it comes to men, and making intelligent choices about relationships with the opposite sex.

As the expression goes, "What's good to you ain't necessarily good for you."
My name is Dora "Peaches" King. I was born in a small town, 50 miles outside of Jackson, Mississippi called Madisonville, population 97, 820, and growing. And this is my story — uncensored and uncut. It's also a testament to how decisions can impact our destiny.

A lot of what I am about to share with you might appear as if the women in my stories were victims of circumstance. But in the end, we do have choices; learning to choose correctly is the key to survival and sanity on the other side.

I believe, that somehow if we were watching our lives unfold from a distance, like looking at a movie or looking at someone else's life, (as we do with our girlfriends who make dumb ass decisions regarding men), we never would have allowed, accepted, tolerated or dealt with the B.S. and the drama encountered by the opposite sex.
Why is it that we cannot see our own chaos but can call the affairs of someone else's life to the letter?
In my story, like the story of many women, there are joys and tragedies. The point is to learn from all of it.

Not to repeat the same mistakes, and to pass that wisdom down to other generations so that they will not perpetuate the same cycles of dysfunction, and learn to define "love" on their own terms. To prevent perpetuating the same cycles and tragedies that too many of us "inherit" as part of our family legacy.

From the day I was born, my life was full of drama, one sad scene after another. But it is my life, and I have to take ownership of it.

Here is my story — the good, bad and the ugly. I hope at the end of it, I will have given you something that will help you to take a look outside of your normal pattern, and learn from my mistakes, and the mistakes of some of the other women in my story. To help spare you the pain and sorrow we experienced-- because Big Momma never told me this would happen! The best place to start is at the beginning, the time in my life when I started to learn who I was; well, during the first part of my life, who I would become was based on the plan that my family mapped out for me.

I know now they did not do this to hurt me; they did have my best in mind. But unfortunately, they didn't realize that to guide me to become the person **they wanted** me to become was not healthy for any of us, or in my best interest. At the time I did not understand that this **was my life**; I had the right to decide who I was going to be, and how I would live it, and with whom I would share my life and my love.

That **YES**, I had the right to choose; that knowledge came later. By the time I finish I will change in many ways; at times and in some situations not knowing myself at all. Who I was, or what I truly need to be okay, happy, and safe!

It appears that my "reality check" bounced! I didn't know that "the key to becoming the person you want to be is to know who you really are!" Big Momma used to tell me that God had a plan for me, for my life. I suppose God did have a plan for me, because there must be a reason why I was spared, I survived to tell my story. Not spared the pain or humiliation that bad love can bring you, but my life was spared, I lived; unlike my sister, my aunt and my cousin. I survived an abusive relationship.

And I learned that domestic violence is not always between a husband and wife. It can be between a boyfriend and girlfriend, an ex-husband and ex-wife, or ex-girlfriend and ex-boyfriend; it can even include someone who you have dated only a couple of months.

That's right, crazy can come in all time frames; there is no formula or format, just straight unpredictable madness! Over the next three decades, I will learn some painful lessons and some powerful truths.

I am still not sure that if my grandmother and my great-aunts had told me the truth about men that I would have avoided the things I went through.

Don't get me wrong, they were wise women, and there was much important information hidden in the many conversations we had as a family. However, my grandmother, aunts and great-aunts left out a **lot** of critical facts about relationships, about life, love, living, making choices, and the consequences of not heeding my own damn advice!

Chapter 1
BACK IN THE DAY

In 1967, I was a junior in high school; but before I dive any deeper into my life story, let me fill you in on a day in the life of Peaches King! My high school years should have been the times of my life, where I would live the carefree existence of a teenage girl. Enjoying each day with no worries, and no problems, other than if my parents will allow me to wear makeup, and what I should wear to the prom.

I wish it had been that easy for me; no self-pity here, just a statement of my truth. Almost since the day I could recognize my own name, I was working hard to prove **something**, to someone in my life. Rather real or imagined, I had to prove to the people around me, that I was smart enough, that I was talented enough, and I was strong enough, to carry the legacy of the family I was born into.

Our living arrangements were unique, my family and mine. —Technically I lived with my mother, but it was my grandmother who raised me. She and my grandfather treated me more like a daughter than a granddaughter. This agreement was decided between my mother and grandparents after I was born. I used to blame the circumstances of my birth for everything that went wrong in my world.

Although the details of my conception did cause a bit of discomfort for me, it was not a real tragedy, just a weak excuse for me to misbehave. And as much as my grandparents spoiled me in an effort to try to make up for my mother's lack of genuine maternal love for me, it did not help me through the issues I had with her.

Later, because I allowed the wound to fester, life gave me a serious ass whipping for that bit of self-pity. ***But, I digress.***

Ours was a handsome family, with strong genes on both sides. It is uncanny how the women favor Big Momma, almost her mirror image, and the men look like Papa, with just a hint of Big Momma thrown in to make it interesting.

Although tall and dark like Papa, they have curly and wavy hair, a legacy of their mother. According to my grandfather, I look like my "grandmother's people," "tall, around 5'9," light skin, with "good hair." I was well built for a girl my age, also attributed to my grandmother's "genes."

Long hair was another family trait; all of the women in our family's hair grew long, naturally. My sisters reveled in this attribute of our family line, but I preferred to wear my hair cut into a short style. *Later I realized this was another form of rebellion against my mother!*
I would drive all the way to Jackson to have my hair done, *(something else my mother didn't approve of);* "there are plenty of good beauticians in Madisonville," she would yell at me, "Why drive all the way to Jackson? Your hair better be all you are getting *done* in Jackson, with your fast behind!"

I was an athlete; a runner, I broke records at my school. I think running helped me to release my anxieties and work through the stress of growing up "King." My mother's take on my looks and ability as an athlete was, "The only thing all of this is doing for you is to encourage your fastness!"

She *was* half right, although I was not having that much fun doing it, I made a dent in the 15-20 year old male population of Madisonville, *(and I wondered why most of the young women my age didn't want to see me coming).*

When that got dull, I found a sweetie in Jackson to amuse me for a time, any excuse to get out of Madisonville for a few hours. My trips to Jackson to see my flavor of the month made my mother crazy mad. We would fight like, *"we are going to the woodshed, and one of us was not going to come out alive!"*

When things got too hot, I would run to my grandparents, and my grandfather would get between us, until one of us backed down.

But in spite of all that prowling around, and constant battles with my mother, I still managed to be in the honor society and president of the student body, during both my junior and senior years in high school. *(An honor held only by one other person in the history of Madison high, my uncle, William)!*

My mother would say, "you better be smart because you aren't good at anything, but chasing boys," this statement goes a long way in describing my relationship with her; *to say it was strained would be an understatement!*

I know that she was the reason why my grandfather gave me anything I wanted, and allowed me to do whatever I wanted. It was his way of trying to make up for my mother's bad behavior toward me, *(throw money at the problem)!*

Aside from my rebellious attitude toward my mother, I was basically a good kid; the problem was that I did not have anyone to truly help me through the difficulty of my relationship with her.

No one in my family seemed to know what to do about it; the ever growing battles of wills that defined our relationship. Papa giving me money to make me feel better was obviously not the answer.

If it were happening twenty years later, I am sure we would have gone to some type of family counseling.

However, this chapter in the King family book of darkness and drama, was during the era when black people didn't go to counseling. We didn't think we needed counseling, we believed that mental health issues and emotional imbalance were a "white people" sickness.

We prayed about it, and handled our problems within the family circle as we all tried, although in vain, not to air our dirty laundry in public. During my unruly teen years, I told myself that it did not matter to me what my mother thought of me. But my anxiety regarding our relationship said otherwise.

My attitude didn't change toward my mother until I went away to college. I don't know if it was being away from her that made me look at our relationship differently; or if it was my own maturity that helped me to realize, that she was acting from a place of pain, and self-hatred. That those emotions were manifesting as dislike for her daughter.

But until that time, when I realized what was happening to her, I tried to make her feel as bad as she made me feel. Our saving grace was my grandparents. Whenever we started to get on each other's nerves, she would either send me, or I would walk out of the house, and go and stay at my grandparent's house, sometimes for weeks.

My grandparent's didn't live far from us, but it was far enough to give us both enough distance to cool off.

I did not understand why she wouldn't allow me to go and live with them. I believe that she thought it would bring me too much joy. She would say, "They spoil you rotten, you need to stay at home with me so that I can keep you grounded!"

I realize that to listen to me describe my life with my family, and our existence in this small town, we sound like *switchblade slinging, 40-ounce drinking, ghetto- neck, waving-rowdy black people,* but that was not the case; far from it. Ours was a pleasant little town, with churches, schools, and quaint little shops along our main street. The neighborhoods were filled with families and beautiful homes.

Most of the people in the area where we lived owned their homes, which was unusual for black people in the south during the 1930s and 1940s. In the 1963, we even started to see a few whites' trickle into our neighborhood, mostly transplants from the North. Papa used to say that they were "Hippies -free thinkers who didn't realize that living next door to black people would lower the value of their property!"

My uncle Anderson would say, "They were smart to invest in a home in *Pinehurst* (the area we lived in). "The houses are twice the size of the homes in most of the "white only" areas, for a lot less money." That was true with the exception of *Forest Hills*, the exclusive "white only" area of town where our mayor lived. The homes in Pinehurst were large and built to stand the test of time. Most of the homes were built by the owners' themselves, or they were on site every day to supervise the work. At that time there was no such thing as cost cutting in property development. Everything was done with quality materials and the proper time was taken to make sure the job was done right.

I learned all of this from listening to my family talk about business.
"Only prejudice was keeping others in the community from seeing the value in living here," said Uncle Anderson. "Besides, with civil rights, things are beginning to change in the south, for the better."

Yes, things were beginning to change, as my uncle said. Between the late 1930s through 1968, Mississippi was at the center of a hotbed of activity surrounding the civil rights movement; close to home the fight for equality also included rural areas of Tennessee and Arkansas.

Because we are tucked away outside of the mainstream of much of the activity, we were not subjected to the **same** dangers and horrors of racism that many black people experienced during that time. Still the small town where I was born was extremely segregated. Although it was a peaceful coexistence with the white community, we were separated.

In 1967, when I was still in high school everyone in our neighborhood went to the all-Negro high school.
My siblings and I all went to Madison High, as did my mother, and her sisters and brothers--my aunts and uncles.
Although at times living in a small town was tedious; it did have its benefits, but extracurricular activities were not one of them. Because the town was off the beaten path and stuck in-between two big cities, we did not possess our own identity. And because many of the descendants of the founding families still lived in the town, and were determined to maintain some semblance of the old world, small town quality of life, it was pretty old fashioned; and sometimes resistant to change.

Often we young people had to invent our own fun and after school traditions. One of the things we all enjoyed was music, dancing to it and being a part of it. In our high school, most everyone was on rotation with the same three male singing groups "the Monotones" "the Cool Gents," and "the Heartbreaker," and two female singing groups, "the Toneetts," and "the Lady Loves."

None of us had expectations of becoming world famous singers, or being discovered in a high school talent show, but it was fun to be on stage and out front, swinging and swaying to the music in perfect harmony. The talented groups were like local celebrities, even playing for paying gigs at nightclubs.

Another sad and frightening tradition was that most everyone married his or her high school sweetheart (once your parents agreed that you could date). *Small town, limited choices!* Other than family drama, I had the normal life of a young Negro, (*okay African American*) - girl growing up in the south in the 1950s, and 60's.

We had the same troubles and challenges as teenagers in the bigger cities- puberty, sex — *to do or not to do*--boys, grades, drugs --*to do or not to do*, and family relationship issues. But because I was a member of the King family, "normal or regular" would not quite describe my life and my experiences growing into an adult. Unlike many black families living in our town at that time, we were "well off" as Papa used to say, sadly I learned that having money didn't solve all of our problems. Sometimes and in some situations, it was the cause of them.

We were a close family, despite our many dysfunctions, we loved each other. Though I would never admit it to anyone out loud, I love my mother, even if I do not **like** her very much! However, the patterns that would shape my family legacy were set in motion long before I was born, before my mother (Sara Lynn King) was born. Everyone called her Lynn, and likely before my grandmother (Ella Mae King) "Big Momma" was born.

The foundation was laid, and until I understood that I had control over my life, that I could make choices regulating what was happening to me. I fell in line and went through the motions like everyone around me.

Trying to find my way, trying to survive the American dreams that were not my own, they were borrowed from television shows, magazines, movies and my families' bad examples.

"NEVER GONNA GIVE YOU UP"

On more than one occasion my grandmother, Big Momma saved my life. Not literally, but for everything that mattered to me, she was there to hold my hand, or cheer me on. I cannot remember a time that she was not there for all of us. Solving problems, or making a fuss over some accomplishment to make us all feel special. She was our anchor; she held our family together, even through the toughest of times.

My grandmother was a beautiful woman, with olive skin and long dark hair that she would wear in a braid twisted around her head in the daytime, and she would let the braid fall down her back at night.

All of her daughters, my mother and her sisters would have her beauty. The women of the King family were known for their good looks and sharp dress.

I also remember that every child and adult in the community called my grandmother Big Momma.

Although she was hardly big in size, she was big in spirit and in thought and courage. Big Momma was the matriarch of the neighborhood.

All of the families in our community relied on Big Momma for everything from recipes, to telling a young girl what she should do when she found herself in ***trouble.*** Whatever the problem or question, Big Momma had the solution or remedy! There was nothing in my young eyes that Big Momma could not do. She was surely my hero!

⌘

    Despite that she only went as far as the 8th grade in school, she seemed to have the knowledge and wisdom to rival any scholar; she didn't need book knowledge. My mother would say "she was a student of hard times".

    The story goes that my grandfather, William King II (Papa) kidnapped my grandmother from her father's house in Little Rock, Arkansas back in 1912, when she was only 13 years old. My Great-grandfather, Big Momma's father, was a white Irishman who was brave enough to marry a woman of color in Arkansas back when the only thing that was more plentiful in the south than cotton was prejudice, racism and segregation.

    My great-grandmother also named Ella was Indian and Black, the combination was quite exotic. It is said that she was a very beautiful woman, although quite petite, according to Papa she could "out-curse and out shoot any man in town!"

    Likely, these *attributes* were survival tools. During that time in American history, being a pretty minority or a woman of color was more dangerous than a blessing. Some of the white farmers in the area kept cabins in the woods where they would make moonshine whiskey.

    My grandmother told us that this toxic liquid would fry their brains, and give them more of an excuse to terrorize the black community.

    They would get drunk and go prowling around in the village where the black people lived *looking for a good time*. Those men knew most of the women who lived there. Likely they worked in their homes during the day as domestics.

They also knew that the black men in the village worked late in the fields or that they had to travel to other towns looking for work, and came home only on the weekends, and the women were alone.

There were times when the women were attacked, beaten; often raped and murdered during these *raids!* They knew the men that attacked them would never be brought to justice or convicted of the crimes, because they were white men.

The women, if they survived the attack, would never be allowed to testify against the men in a court of law. At that time in the south, the law would not allow a black person to testify against a white person for any crime, even rape and murder.

They knew there would be no justice, so they had to learn to protect themselves.

Big Momma used to also tell us that her mother was a healer in the village where she was born. She taught Big Momma about plants and herbs, and gave her home remedies for every illness or affliction from colic to snake bites. There was only one doctor in the community where Big Momma's mother lived that would treat her people.

Her family often had to rely on their own healers and remedies when someone was sick or injured, and the doctor was away treating other patients in the town; learning to heal others was a necessity for her.

Big Momma's father swore to kill my grandfather if he caught up with him for stealing Little Ella away. Papa was tough, but he was no fool. He was not about to tussle with Big Momma's father, although he was not afraid, a physical confrontation with a white man in Arkansas in 1912, was not smart or safe, even more so, if the man was the father of your new wife. Big Momma's age was not as much a problem for her father as the disrespect of taking her, when her family didn't give their approval for them to marry. To avoid a run in with her father, Papa moved his new young wife far away from Little Rock to Madisonville Mississippi.

Because of that separation, to this day, we know very little about my grandmother's family and history; only the short stories and the things that she could remember about her life with her parents.

When she and Papa finally settled in Mississippi, it seemed that almost immediately they began to have children, seven in all. I am told that one daughter died as a small child. Looking back, it is not that far from Little Rock to Mississippi, only about 200 miles.

However, I guess back then when there was no internet, and no GPS to track them, no Facebook or Instagram to tell everyone your business and your whereabouts; it was easy to escape into a small town, even if they were only a few hundred miles away.

Big Momma never saw or spoke with her family again. Not one visit or phone call.
I thought that it was because she was so young when she left, that she wouldn't know how to find them.

My mother's sister, my Aunt Ella (named for Big Momma's mother), told me that Papa wouldn't let her go home, that he would get messages from people that he kept in contact with back in Little Rock, and they would give him information about what was going on there.

It is rumored that he even went back a few times to see **his** parents and family, but would not tell Big Momma about the visits. When Big Momma's mother was sick and dying, he didn't tell her. When her father died asking for his baby girl, he didn't tell her. He kept up the lie that it was too dangerous to contact her family or go back to Arkansas.

I never understood why he did this. My uncles said it was for "her own protection," yeah right! I believe it was another part of his ultimate control over her!

I could not believe that my grandfather could be so cruel and unfair; with us, he was always warm and caring. "When Papa was a young man he was different," Aunt Ella would say. If Big Momma suspected that it was all a lie, that enough time had passed and her parents were not angry anymore, that they simply wanted to see their daughter again, she never let on. She settled into her life with her husband, and continued to survive under Papa's rules.

My grandfather was a house painter by trade. The men in the King family had been house painters for as long as I could remember. It was a profession passed down to him from his father and grandfather.

Papa's grandfather would say, "Arkansas has enough farmers." Back when they started the business in 1882, although it was still a frontier town; Arkansas was growing and building, "someone is going to need to paint and decorate the new homes and businesses that are springing up all over Pulaski County."

⌘

Papa did not have much more education than Big Momma, but he was a savvy businessman and was very successful. My grandfather was as talented a house "decorator" as his father and grandfather.

A testament to his talent was that although he started his business in Mississippi in 1914 -- Papa managed to have quite a bit of work in the "white only" part of town. Madisonville was growing and developing, but was extremely segregated –his talent helped him avoid those barriers.

Perhaps it was luck, and talent, or maybe it was being in the right place at the right time, but his business grew quickly. His income more than provided for his family, he even owned the house he and Big Momma lived in. For a black man in Mississippi in the 1900s, that was quite an accomplishment!

My grandfather started his business with two work trucks that had his business name painted on the side, **King's Decorating**. He made enough money to hire other men to work with him, with a crew he could hire out for several jobs at one time. Papa said he worked hard as he did so that his wife didn't need to work. With her lack of education, he realized the only work she would get was as a domestic.

Papa would always say, "The only house my wife was going to clean is mine!"
For my grandfather, that was the purpose of her life with Him; Big Momma stayed home to take care of *his* home and the children.

She could not read well and she could barely write her name. In spite of this shortcoming, somehow she managed to budget the money she received from Papa to pay the bills, buy the grocery that she didn't grow in her garden, and buy clothing for herself and the children, along with taking care of any other expenses, they might have.

As the children grew older, they would help her with these things; helping manage the household finances and keeping records of bills, or whatever was required for running a home the size of theirs; like insurance papers, documentation on the purchase or selling of livestock, medical bills, etc.

Because Papa made all the money, he would dictate to her how she was to spend the money **he** made. Often the money he allotted for housekeeping would fall short if the children needed something extra; things like new shoes when they already had one pair, which Papa thought was enough, or a new dress for a school dance for the girls, or a new suit for graduation for the boys.

Without Papa knowing, Big Momma would bake for the neighbors, as well as wash and iron their clothing for extra money. She would tell him that Miss Anita, her friend who lived three miles down the road, was the one doing the baking and ironing, and she was out helping her friend, if he got home and she was out—*that is if she didn't beat Papa home from making a delivery!* She could not tell him the truth about what she was doing, because she knew how he felt about her working or doing any type of "labor" for someone outside of him, even if she did have a good reason.

Big Momma and her friend were forced to hatch a plan to get her out of the house, when she needed to work.

Miss Anita was her partner in crime, and would agree to drive her around to help her to make the money she needed. Big Momma's luxuries were few; the extra money was always intended for something for the children.

For her own enjoyment, she would listen to her "stories" and her "music shows" on the radio each afternoon while she did her washing, ironing, cooking and cleaning. She and Papa had a large house.

Papa added rooms to the house every year until it was a small mansion. Their house sat on 20 acres of land. It was one of the first houses in our area to have indoor plumbing and toilets. Big Momma called it a *water closet*.

They had a huge kitchen and pantry, five bedrooms, a formal dining room and living room, along with a sitting room off of the master bedroom. Papa had an office at the house or *a study*, as Aunt Jamie would call it, because he was always working. Big Momma managed the house all by-herself. Although they could afford a housekeeper to assist her with the housework; Big Momma was not willing to "share her space with another grown woman that was not family!"

Her exercise was walking the five miles to the schoolhouse and back, to pick up the children each day. She did not drive, Papa would not teach her. Papa said she did not need to drive, "she had him to take her everywhere she wanted to go." When he was not working, Papa would drive her to the grocery store, or pharmacy and anywhere else she had to go as long as it was part of her "wifely duties."

For personal activities like church and her women's group, one of her friends would drive her. When the boys grew older, it was their job to take their mother to her extracurricular activities, which Papa felt these activities took her away from her family and her duties as his wife.

Big Momma didn't oppose Papa on many issues, most of the time things went his way, whether she agreed with him or not. But for this she held her ground. This was important to her, she didn't back down.

Eventually he allowed her these few outside pleasures. If he was working late or across town when she had to go somewhere too far to walk that was related to completing her chores, he allowed our neighbor, and Big Momma's best friend Miss Anita to drive her to run errands.

⌘

Miss Anita was from Madisonville, born and raised. Like Big Momma, she had the respect of the community. She was a big burly woman, with a loud voice and an equally loud and infectious laugh. She smoked a pipe, and wore a sundress every day, winter or summer.

Rumor has it, her husband died, and she collected money from a large insurance policy after his death.
The town gossip was that she killed him, that during an argument he made the mistake of slapping her, a week later he was dead of a heart attack.

People said that she put rat poison in his food. Although it was never proven, no one, man or woman messed with Miss Anita, not even Papa. So, when she said that she needed Big Momma to help her make a delivery, Big Momma helped her make a delivery.

Papa did not argue about it. He had no idea the women were actually working a side job behind his back. Big Momma would tell him that she should give Miss Anita money on her gas for taking her around when he could not. If he started to protest about the gas money, she would remind him that the woman was doing both of them a favor.

For her to have her chores done before he got home, and have his dinner on the table, sometimes she would need Miss Anita's help. Of Course, Miss Anita did not ask Big Momma for money, she wanted to help her; she would never take money from her. My mother and her sisters would say that Big Momma was burying that money in the back yard. She would say that it was her *just in case money*.

One of the lessons Big Momma would say to us was *"not to let the left hand know what the right hand is doing."* Always have your own money in case of an emergency."
But she never said what type of emergency that we should prepare for. "Just try to put a little something away for yourself." Although my grandfather was strict and he kept a tight hand on the purse with Big Momma, his family lived well and was comfortable. It seemed to be a nice existence.

But for me, something more was happening; there was sadness around Big Momma that I could not identify. Although I never saw her cry, as a child, I remember Big Momma having sad eyes. She would often sit and stare out of the window for hours. When I asked what she was thinking about, she would say, *"I am thinking about what if."*

I didn't know at the time that *what if* meant; what if she never married my grandfather, or never left her parents behind? What if she had finished school, and learned how to drive? What if her life had been different? If her choices were different than the ones she made that brought her to this place in her life.

So far away from her family, and her history, all of her choices taken away from her, what if it was different? "No need in dreaming" she would then say, "life is what it is today and that is all there is until tomorrow!"

Then moving as if she was carrying the weight of the world, she would get back to her chores.

You see, what Big Momma didn't tell me was that Papa was often violent and abusive. He would drink and come home fussing and complaining about anything and everything.

He would hit her, and beat her for years until his sons were too big to allow him to abuse their mother. Then they would beat *him* when he was drunk and trying to fight with her.

This was a weekly series of events in the home of my grandparents; according to my mother and aunts, the fighting, pain, fear and anger were a regular part of their life. Because Big Momma didn't drive, she had no way to leave. Miss Anita offered to take her away, to take her anywhere her *just in case money* would carry her.

But as far as she would go was to Miss Anita's house for a few hours. She never considered leaving him after a fight, no matter how violent she would stay; because of the children-because he was sorry-because she loved her husband and "when he wasn't drunk and being abusive he was a good man!" You see in Big Momma's day, a man providing for his family, paying the bills and having a nice house was something no woman walked away from.

But I believe the real reason she didn't leave was because she didn't know how to live on her own. My grandfather raised her; she was 13 years old when she was taken away from her home. Big Momma knew no other way of life.

This life was all she had, her family here with Papa, taking care of him and the children. I also found out later, as I was listening in on my mother and her sister's talk about our family, that Papa had *several children* by other women in our town and neighboring towns. This was one reason he did not want Big Momma to learn to drive, he didn't want her to find out about all of his wrongdoing!

I could not believe it. First the fighting and now this! I was hurt, disappointed, and so angry with him for betraying our family in this way. I asked my aunt Ella if these things were true, "had Papa actually cheated on Big Momma!" "Oh yes, "she would say, "and Big Momma did not take it lying down!"

My aunt said that in her day Big Momma had "bitched slapped" many a "heifer" that confronted her about Papa. Women coming to the house to let Big Momma know that "he was leaving her for them!"

Big Momma would say, "What he did away from home was his business," but "those bitches were not going to get in her face." Big Momma would beat the women down for coming to her house, and then jump on Papa when he got home, because he was allowing his "street business to come to her door!" When my mother and her sisters would tell these stories to us when we were little children, they would laugh and laugh at the antics of Big Momma and cheating Papa!

Before she became ill, Big Momma would talk about her life and often she would laugh herself. I never knew if it was because of the irony or to keep from crying.

When we were children, we would listen and laugh with them, not thinking for one minute there was something wrong with this story. Not knowing better than to laugh about abuse.

Not knowing any better than to laugh about the pain that Big Momma must have been in, or what she might have been going through emotionally because of the abuse.

Big Momma was tough and she fought; she fought the other women **and** Papa. But she was simply a woman, trying to raise her family under less than stellar conditions. She must have felt pain during those times, and maybe even fear and humiliation, but still, she stayed.

I wonder if she knew deep down, that by staying with him all those years, that by choosing to keep her home and family intact, in spite of my grandfather's abusive behavior, that she was also teaching her children and grandchildren, that this was the way of life and relationships.

That laughing made it not so serious, that it was okay if you could laugh, right? As the years passed and they both grew older, Papa began to change, not as much fighting and he couldn't get around well. Arthritis made it difficult for him to walk. After a time driving was out of the question too. When it got hard for him to get around, we did not hear much more about the other women and families.

Knowing Papa, I am sure that there were "arrangements" made for them. As bad as he was, he would provide for his family, **all of them**! He would tell us, "If you see young people who look like the King family, ask them about who their people are they might be related to us!"
Related! You mean like an aunt or uncle? Needless to say, we did not look for those people, we had enough drama in our family - we were not about to go trolling for new problems! Then Papa began to forget, as if his consciousness could not take the guilt anymore, he began to forget the past; lost to dementia, it took away his memories.

Now without Big Momma, he couldn't eat, dress himself, or even go to the bathroom on his own to relieve himself. As if she had not suffered enough, **now** she had to care for the man who abused her for most of her life.

If she was feeling any resentment she never let on. She just continued to look after him, the way she always had, until the day he died.

⌘

    Life with Big Momma was always interesting, everyday a new experience or discovery! She would teach us how to keep our hair strong with oils and herbs that were made in her kitchen. She taught us how to keep our skin soft and supple, also with homemade remedies.

    We learned how to bake the best sweet potato pie in the county, and how to cut up and fry a chicken to perfection, but she never talked to us about abuse.

    Although she lived with abuse and violence throughout her marriage, she said nothing about smart dating choices, or what makes a healthy relationship. Nothing about what to look for in a man other than his having a "good job" is important.

    My aunts would say that Big Momma did not know if what was happening between her and Papa was bad or good, for her *it was marriage*!

    Besides, where would she learn the difference? Her mother was not a part of her life. Likely, her friends offered their opinions, and told her that Papa was wrong to do the things he did to her.

    But there was never any true education for her about relationship etiquette. Nor any explanation of what male and female relationship interaction should be.

    Other than what she could remember from her life with her family, which she would never talk much about, where would she learn about living as husband and wife? *There was no manual given out at birth you know!*

    We often wondered if there was another reason why she was willing to leave her parents and family behind at such a young age. Was there something more behind her choice besides blind love?

Big Momma's teachings and lectures covered a vast array of topics. But she never spoke a word about how a man should treat us as women; nothing about respect or partnership, but only that "when it came to men, the women in our family were cursed," and that *"none of us would ever have a happily ever-after with a man!"* This revelation leads me to believe even more that Big Momma's mother or her aunts, (her mother's sisters), might also be in abusive relationships with men.

This might explain her willingness to stay with Papa, although his behavior toward her was so dreadful.

Her cryptic statement about women in our family and our sad destiny concerning relationships was all we could ever get out of her in reference to sex and marriage. Or any other issues involving men, and why men are the way they are with the woman they love. So, like Big Momma, our lessons regarding relationships came from trial and error, *lots and lots of error!*

"WHEN LIFE GIVES YOU LEMONS"

My mother and her sisters were close growing up, they were sister-friends. They were raised to take care of each other, and never put anyone before family.

In spite of the fighting and abuse they witnessed as children between their parents, Papa never abused any of them. Unlike most abusive men **who beat his wife and the kids**, Papa never abused any of his children, or his grandchildren; never any discipline that was more than normal punishments and whippings. I often wondered if that was another reason why she never left him, "not even for one full day" my mother would say to us.

Maybe she thought then, as many women in abusive relationship still believe today, that the problem is with her, that **she** needs to be the one to make the changes **in her** behavior. And as long as he is only hitting her, and leaving the children alone, this life is tolerable!

There were four King Sisters, and they went everyplace together, parties, school functions, dates, everyplace. They were like one person, with four different personalities. The older three girls were also the protectors of the baby girl, Bertha Sue- also known as- "Bee."

Bertha Sue is the one who everyone says I take after. She was considered the pretty one, though they all were beautiful. I guess Aunt Bee had that extra something special!
She surely knew her own mind, and would give you a piece of it in a second. *I am sure that is the part of her personality they are comparing to me!*

Aunt Bee's passion was beauty; she was always doing someone's hair and makeup; for her sisters and the other girls at the school. Everyone and anyone in town (black or white) who wanted a great look for a party or special occasion went to my Aunt Bee; she was the ultimate "kitchen beautician."

Her family, including Papa, thought she would want to go to beauty culture school and work in a beauty shop in Madisonville, or perhaps open a beauty salon business.

Papa had the money, and was willing to give her whatever she wanted. As abusive as he was with Big Momma, he loved his children and would do anything for them; strange how that was. Papa swore until the day that he died, "He loved his wife and family," that his behavior was not to hurt her, "but to protect her!" Although Bee did attend beauty school and graduated with flying colors, working in Madisonville was not at all on her life's list of things to do.

Bee wanted out of Madisonville. She wanted to move to St. Louis, *the big city* and find her fame and fortune there.

When Bee told her family that she wanted to move to the city with a girlfriend, (Dolly Anderson), her family did not offer the resistance she feared they would. Dolly was another smart girl from Madisonville; she was going to school in St. Louis to become a teacher. She invited Bee to come with her, so that she could make a go of being a professional stylist.

Dolly had family in St. Louis; she was going to help Bee get a job working in her aunt's *beauty shop*, until she could decide if the beauty business was really what she wanted to do. Dolly's aunt had seen Aunt Bee's work when she came home to visit her family in Madisonville. She liked what she saw in Bee, she was happy to hire her as a shampoo girl, train her, and help her to develop her craft.

To everyone's surprise Papa didn't object. However, Big Momma did not want her to go. She said that she kept having dreams about Bee, that she saw her in a dream and she appeared to be falling. She could not make sense of the dream; she said that when the time grew closer for Bee to leave, Big Momma's dream came more often.

She did not know what to make of it — Big Momma's grandmother was said to have a *Gift*. My mother would say that Big Momma had it too, that she could sense things. And she had a feeling of dread about Aunt Bee moving away from home. But her husband and children attributed her feeling to simply not wanting her daughter to leave.

Of course, her children and her husband would say Big Momma's dreams were crazy, and always laughed them off, telling her that she was being overly protective.

⌘

    Big Momma was always worrying over her children, but they were as safe in our small town as anywhere. I believe the fear of someone hurting her children, was the after effect of being taken away from her own family at such a young age.

    Although she agreed to leave with Papa, her family didn't know that she was gone until it was too late to stop her. The fact was no one from Madisonville would dare try to harm one of William King's children, or grandchildren. My grandfather had the respect of the community. Not only was he known as a successful businessman; he was also known for exacting revenge on anyone who tried to steal from him, or take advantage of him in business.

    He had a reputation for being tough in business and in the street. We would hear him say, "A black man in Mississippi has to protect his family, and everyone in town should know that he will do whatever it takes, to make that happen. No matter if the issue was with a black man or a white man, respect must be demanded to survive; a man cannot let race decide how he will be treated, in any situation."

    Other than a bad date or two, not much happened to any of the children outside of the family compound, while they were growing up King!
The girls also had their brothers to make sure that no boy disrespected or tried to take advantage of them.

    They were tough, and no nonsense like their father, and the people in our town knew it. No doubt about it, don't mess with the Kings... it will not end well for you!

My grandfather was a leader in the community and a pioneer without ever trying to be one. In his youth, he was simply trying to survive and provide for his family.

But he influenced many black people in the town to start businesses, and educate their children. He would say "We need to rely on our own resources to live, and never be at the mercies of others for your survival."

His reputation for leadership, along with Papa being one of the few black business owners in the community, caused him to be somewhat of a celebrity in town, his children were as well.

Of course it was assumed that the boys would follow in the footsteps of their father, and would have power and money one day. So, the girls in the neighborhood would fall all over them, trying to be the chosen one.

But it was not to happen; much to the dismay of the unmarried women in our town, neither of the King sons married until they came home from the Korean War in 1951 and 52, and to women they met while away at school.

Although they dated more than their share of young women in town, my uncles didn't choose wives until they both went away to college, at Fisk University in Nashville Tennessee in 1939 and 1940. While the ladies who would later become their wives, went to Knoxville College also in Tennessee.

Meeting interesting men was the other reason Aunt Bee wanted to leave town, none of the men here were exciting or interesting enough for her; and it didn't help that she had known most of them all of her life.

Billy James was one boy in particular that was very smitten with Aunt Bee. He was an apprentice to Papa in his house painting business, and according to Papa, "he had lots of potential."

It would have made Papa happy to see Billy and Aunt Bee married. Although they dated for a while after high School, behind his back Aunt Bee would call Billy, "*a slow moving country hick*" and that she would "*gouge out her own eyes before she married anyone that dull!*"

To the heartbreak of Big Momma, Bee moved to St. Louis with her father's blessing. Papa wanted to drive her, but she would have none of it. She was 23 years old and a grown woman. She wanted to start her new life on her own terms. Bee had an old Oldsmobile that Papa bought her for a high school graduation present, and she wanted to drive herself and her friend to St. Louis.

Since the girls didn't want Papa to drive them, he elected my uncle's William and Anderson to drive with them. It was more than 400 miles, and Big Momma was putting her foot down about the young women driving that distance alone. In 1945, black people traveling by car had to stay in a **"colored only"** hotel if the drive was a lengthy one.

There were a few decent hotels in certain parts of the country, but not many. Sometimes Negro families found lodging at a boarding house so they could take a break while traveling, or they would make contact with family friends along the way, that would offer shelter while on the road.

Often they would sleep in the car. That was fine for men traveling alone, but for young women it was dangerous. If the men were with them, they could drive straight through, and not worry about having to stop. It was safer for them. Once they arrived in St. Louis, Dolly's aunt had a small one-bedroom apartment over her *beauty shop*, where she was allowing the young women to stay, for very little rent.

Dolly and Bee would pay the rent together, they were roommates-but I am certain that without the girl's knowing it, Papa gave Dolly's aunt money for their rent and living expenses; again, safety was an issue.

Dolly had not started to work yet, and Bee was planning to live off of the money she saved from doing hair for friends and family before she left Madisonville. That was all the money she had until she began to make money as a shampoo girl, at the beauty shop. But that money would not be enough to pay all of her living expenses for quite some time.

If they wanted to look for an apartment apart from Dolly's aunt, because this was the 1940s, the girls would be restricted to live in the 'Colored Only" areas in different parts of St. Louis. Likely most of the apartments in the city that they could afford would not be in the nicer part of town.

Although Papa wanted to encourage her independence, he was going to make sure that she would have enough money to live on comfortably. Through Dolly's aunt, he could assist her, until she made enough money to live on her own.

Finally the time came for them to leave. Bee did not want a lot of fanfare at her departure, mostly because she didn't want to see Big Momma cry.

They were up at first light to hit the road. My uncle's said goodbye to their girlfriends and left with Aunt Bee and her friend for St. Louis. They were going to take the train back home, but not before purchasing gifts for their lady friends while in the city.

Aunt Bee had impeccable taste in clothing, and everything else (but men), so she was charged with choosing the gifts. Bee was so excited about her new life she could hardly stand it; she could not wait for her adventure to begin!

Why shouldn't she be excited? She was living her dream. She was young, talented and beautiful; she had her whole life to look forward to, and this was just the beginning.

"EVERY BODY WANTS TO RULE THE WORLD"

Aunt Bee was right about moving to the city. She blossomed as a hair stylist and makeup artist. Dolly's aunt recognized her exceptional talent and helped her along, training her in the proper styling techniques and tools of the trade.

By the time she had her own styling station a year later, she had a full client list, along with outside work for weddings, parties and even funerals; news of the talented and pretty "colored girl" in town spread fast.

It wasn't long before the white ladies that lived in one of the more exclusive "white' only" part of town known as *Beverly-Glen*, heard about her talents through their maids and cooks, and began to have her come to their home to do hair and makeup for special occasions.

She was so busy with the extra work she almost did not have time for her regular customers. But Bee was determined, she was finally living her dream, as challenging as it was at times, she made it work.

With all of that going on in her life, she still made time to party and have fun with her friends! Someone on the block was always celebrating some event; the invitations for parties were endless. Although she went out a lot and was having a good time, Bee was not the type of woman who would attract many women friends. It was not because of a lack of personality; her looks, background, and quick success, made some of the other stylists less than friendly toward her.

But she was never bored or lonely. She was still Dolly's friend and roommate. And she also had a couple of other women friends she hung out with. But her closest friend besides Dolly, was a cross dresser who worked in the shop with her named Trudi. Miss Trudi to the common people!

Miss Trudi was as talented as Aunt Bee styling hair and doing makeup; however, she was not quite as successful as Bee, "because most people don't understand her," Aunt Bee would say. Aunt Bee liked Trudi because she said that Trudi was true to who she was, that she did not try to hide her sexuality, and she was not ashamed to be herself.

Aunt Bee would talk about how talented Trudi was with her sisters when she called home to fill them in on her latest adventure. She told them that Trudi could style a head of hair! Cut it, color it, tease it, all while chain-smoking a pack of Camel cigarettes and not drop a curl!

To the amusement of them all, somehow Miss Trudi managed to be invited to the biggest events in town. Not just any party or affairs, but events that were attended by celebrities, politicians, and other high profile personalities in the city. When the Negro League Baseball team was in town playing a game, Aunt Bee, Trudi and friends were invited. They all went to the game **and** the after party.

Aunt Bee and Dolly never asked Trudi how she managed to make such important friends, and Miss Trudi never volunteered the information. In fact, that was another thing that Bee loved about Miss Trudi; she was as loyal as any "female" friend she ever had.

She said that she could tell Miss Trudi all of her dreams and fears, and like many women, she never tried to use it against her, or use the information later to shame her because of jealousy; "she was true blue!"

No matter how busy she was, Aunt Bee also always managed to find time for men! The men came and went in droves. Some good ones, too many bad ones, but none that brought any real love into Aunt Bee's life, or so she thought, until she met Brad.

⌘

Bradley Hastings was the brother of one of her white clients. He was smitten with Bee the first time he saw her at his home, after she finished styling his mother and sister, for a charity event they were hosting.

One evening after she was finished with her work, he caught up to her as she was leaving. He told her, "he had never seen a woman as beautiful as she, and "she won his heart the moment he laid eyes on her."

He made Bee promise to have dinner with him the very next evening. That dinner date changed her life. Bee and Bradley were an instant item, they were inseparable; for months they went everyplace together.

If his family knew about the relationship they never complained or confronted her about it. Since Bee was a colored girl, surely they thought it would never become serious, just a temporary amusement, "a passing fancy for Bradley!"

Bee on the other hand felt that *she* had hit the jackpot! *She*, thought this was further confirmation, that she made the right choice in leaving Madisonville. Her career could not be going better, and there were no men like Brad back home in Mississippi! With his charm, wealth and influence, he wined and dined her all over town.

He took her to restaurants and nightclubs that she never could have gotten into without him, and some she could not get into even with him.

They spent most of their time partying on the Negro side of town, because of the segregation and racism in the city; it was easier. But even there it was often still a problem.

Brad was rich, handsome and white. Although they were further north than Mississippi when they started dating in 1947- things were changing. But the world was still not readily accepting of interracial couples.

There were other issues with Bee and Bradley beside racism starting to surface. The relationship was not turning out to be the dream come true Bee wished for. With all the outside trappings Brad brought with him, he had a dark secret. In-between the wining and dining, he had the habit of slapping my aunt around. Sometimes he would beat her so badly she could not go to work. During those times, she could count on Miss Trudi to take on her work that she could not miss- *that is if the client would accept Miss Trudi.*

Many times Trudi would have to service her white clients as well, because Bee couldn't afford to not show up for an appointment. The client either didn't notice anything different about Miss Trudi, because Trudi was always impeccably styled herself; and they did not know that she was a Transgender male, or because the occasion was so important, the customer just didn't care.

If handling all of that was not enough of a challenge for her, Aunt Bee began to lose clients because of her constant "accidents" or string of sudden "illnesses" that caused her to miss so many of her regular appointments.

Trudi covered many of her duties, but she could only do so much. Although Trudi was good, her customers wanted Bee to service them. And these excuses were not enough anymore.

Back in the 1940's and early 50's there was no definition of relationship violence. There was not even a word for men who beat their girlfriends, except **mean.** There was no dating violence awareness or information. Nothing to warn women that the man she is involved with could one day harm her.

That physical fighting and name-calling was not a normal part of relationship behavior. Likely, because of their racial situation, *(her being black and he white)* she could not call the police. Unfortunately, in that era, the thought of calling the police never entered her head.

It was *unheard* of back then to call the police during a couple's fight or argument, even if they were the same nationality and background. If they were a married couple, usually the male relatives of the victim "took care of the situation." Depending on how serious the beating and the mentality of the family, the resolution could be anywhere from the victim moving home with her family, or the abuser being beaten, or even killed in retaliation by the victim's family.

Like most violent relationships, the beatings from Brad did not get better, they got worse. Because my aunt was such fair skin color, it took weeks for the bruises to heal.

Bee was embarrassed, she didn't want anyone to see her this way, she would tell her friends and coworkers that she was ill, to avoid seeing them.

Or that she had an accident of some kind to explain the bruises or to hide them until they had time to heal. Sometimes she said that she had been clumsy, "tripped and injured herself falling down the stairs, or rushing around and "not looking where she was going, she walked into a door."

After months of this, Bee had run out of excuses for all of the "accidents" and mishaps she claimed to have, and didn't know what to say to the people around her anymore. It was easier for her to try and come up with a lie than to admit that she had been beaten.

Even though she tried to hide the truth, everyone knew what was going on; it was a small community and there were not many secrets; many of the other stylists' felt that Bee got what she deserved for being with a white man.

That she had stepped outside of her place and her *"diktee -high tone ways"* had gotten her in trouble. They were jealous of her anyway, and wanted Dolly's aunt to let her go. Dolly's aunt stood firm, she would not do it. Bee's work brought prestige to her beauty shop and because she was Dolly's friend, she considered her family.

However, she also knew that something needed to change, or my aunt would not survive her relationship with Brad. Today it would be considered an intervention. Trudi, Dolly and her aunt, developed a plan to keep Brad away from Aunt Bee until they could talk some sense into her.

Because he had to pass the shop door to get to their apartment; during working hours either Trudi, or Dolly's aunt would look out for him, and tell him she was not at home. If he insisted on checking himself, they agreed not to let him pass. Brad was not slow or stupid, he figured out quickly what was going on with the women.

One afternoon when they would not allow him to pass, he threatened Dolly's aunt, forcing Miss Trudi to become *"Mr. Tony,"* to stop him!

They all knew that they could not keep this up forever. Bee had to come to her senses and break up with this man. Break it off before someone got hurt, and according to Trudi, "that was going to be Brad!"

Of course, Papa and Big Momma knew nothing about what was happening in St. Louis. Bee only told them about her success and good times. Because of her bruises and injuries, she had not been home in months. And Papa would have hit the roof if he knew that Bee was dating a white man!

Not because of the issues of race, but because at this time in our history, it could have been dangerous for them both. Her friends kept her secret from her family, with the understanding that she would break it off with Bradley, before it was too late.

With the help of her friends, Bee planned for the day she would tell Bradley that it was over between them. Because the only telephone was in the beauty shop, she would call him from there, with her friends on hand to offer moral support. During that era it was not uncommon if black people didn't have a telephone in their house or apartment; they would use the phone in businesses, or public places.

One evening after the shop was closed and everyone had gone home, with the exception of Trudi, Dolly, her aunt and Aunt Bee, she made the call.

When she finished talking with Brad, she told them all he seemed to take the breakup well. Bee told him that her decision to end the relationship was about race, not because of their relationship issues. She told him that her family would not understand or approve of their being together.

Bee was certain that her father and brothers would not like the fact that her boyfriend was white; however she made that part of her story up. Bee felt she had to say this to Brad because she knew he would not accept that she was leaving him because of the violence, and beatings.

She knew that in Bradley's mind, the fighting was not a problem because he was always sorry afterwards. *"After all, he bought her beautiful gifts, and flowers to make up, so she couldn't be upset and want to break it off with him because of that,"* so she had to invent another reason.

Miss Trudi commented, "I do not understand how a man could beat the hell out of his wife or girlfriend; and then bring her a damn bouquet of flowers. And think that it would make up for the black eyes and bruises, pain and humiliation, of being abused by a man who has promised to love you, take care of you, and protect you. When actually the thing you need protecting from is his ass! If it was me, I would take those flowers and beat the hell out of him with them!"

Of course, everyone was elated that Bee followed through on her promise to break up with Bradley. None of her friends wanted to see her hurt, they all knew that even if the beatings did stop, this was St. Louis, Missouri in 1948, what possibility of a future together did they actually have, Bee had to be smart.

She knew in her heart that ending the relationship was the best thing for her. Besides, she had to be honest with herself regarding how she really felt about him--did she love **him**, or what he represented?

They all laughed at Miss Trudi's comments, but they knew deep down that there was nothing funny about abuse. Over the course of the three years that Bee had been in St. Louis, she lost at least two clients to domestic violence deaths. One of the women in the area, who was abused by her husband, was killed when he ran over her with a car.

Her husband happen to see her talking with a man in front of the grocery store, as it turned out, the man was an old friend of her family, not a lover! No, there was nothing funny about abuse. Aunt Bee had grown up in a home where it was common to see her father beat her mother.

She swore as a child that when she grew up, no man would ever hit her like that--that **her** husband was going to love her and treat her like a queen!

Funny what you will put up with when you think you love someone!

"IN MY NEXT LIFE I HOPE I AM NOT A GIRL"

After her breakup with Bradley, everything went back to business as usual. Aunt Bee was back to working her regular hours. No sudden illnesses to take her away from the job she loved so much. Word spreads that she was back consistently at the shop now; so many of the clients that she lost came back.

To her surprise, some of the women in Beverly-Glen wanted Aunt Bee **and** Miss Trudi to come and work on their hair and make-up together. As it happened, during Bee's absence some of the clients were taken with Trudi and her talents. No one-made issues of whether she was male or female, but that she was a talented stylist, and they liked her work!

Her dream was back on track. When Dolly finished school, she landed a job teaching second grade in the school for colored children. Aunt Bee would drop her off at the school on her way to the shop, and was finished working in time to pick her up at the end of the school day.

They moved out of the apartment over the beauty shop right after her break up with Bradley.
Miss Trudi thought it would be safer if she made a clean break, and moved somewhere he could not find her, just in case he decided to come and look for her.

With Dolly's new job, now they were making enough money to rent a nicer apartment. Bee and Dolly could move into a two-bedroom apartment in the colored only part of downtown.

Yes, things were looking up again. Aunt Bee was still a little apprehensive about dating; she did not trust her judgment regarding men right now. Therefore, the trio kept mostly to themselves, and was just out to have a good time, no men in the picture. Single and happy about it, Bee was back to going to the wonderful parties Miss Trudi got them into, back to developing her craft and building her career, planning for the future.

Back to normal! She even managed to take a trip home. Papa and Big Momma were so happy to see her. Big Momma planned a welcome home party and prepared a huge feast for her visit. All of Aunt Bee's old friends showed up to see her.

My mother said that likely, many were coming not to just say hello, but they wanted to see if she had really made it, or if Big Momma and Papa were making up the stories about her success. The 1940s and early 50s was not an easy time for black people when it came to having careers, or owning businesses. In this part of the south, many were lucky to have a decent job, let alone realize the dream of a career.

Blacks, particularly in the South, faced discrimination in jobs and housing, and were often denied their constitutional right to vote. Some states had curfews for African Americans, and sometimes they were restricted from even working in the same room as whites.

So a young girl moving to the big city, to find her fame and fortune was usually a sad dream, often too difficult a process for her to navigate alone-- many who tried returned home shortly after they left, because success was fleeting.

Mostly her true friends wanted to say hello to the successful city girl! And wish her well on her return back to St. Louis. Their last night in town, Bee, along with her sisters, Dolly, Trudi, and some of her friends from town, went out to a nightclub in an area of the city that we call, *The Bottoms*. The place was not more than a hole- in- the- wall, but the music was good and the drinks were strong and cheap.

Many of the young black people in the area went there to have a good time, and so did the young whites in the town, and the surrounding college towns.

It was like a forbidden fruit for them, partying with Negros, and listening to "colored music!" There were no rules in this place, other than- *no shooting, no fighting and no stealing;* or the owners would deal with that person harshly. People of all races, all ages, and income levels went there to let their hair down on Friday and Saturday nights!

As tight as it was in this small and steaming-hot nightclub, along with the mixture of cultures, it should have been a recipe for trouble, a powder keg waiting to explode; however, there was very little trouble in this establishment. The races got along better down here than anywhere in town. The climate of the club was regulated by the no-nonsense attitude of the owner and his partners.

The owner was a World War II veteran, who kept an arsenal of guns behind the bar counter; his friends were somewhat of a security team, also visibly armed.
I guess it made sense that no one wanted to test them, to see if they would actually shoot someone who got out of line, as they threatened to do before the start of each show.

Bee, Dolly, Miss Trudi and crew made it home just before dawn, which didn't leave them much time to prepare for their drive back to St. Louis, say goodbye to her family, and eat the big breakfast Big Momma prepared for them.

An added surprise was that Papa gave Aunt Bee money to help her buy a new car. That old Oldsmobile was not going to be safe for her driving back and forth, between Missouri and Mississippi. Papa wanted his baby girl to come home often; and he was going to insure she could do so, without fear of her breaking down on the road.

She protested of course, because she wanted to use her own money to buy a car. With encouragement from Big Momma not to hurt his feelings, she took the money and promised to pay him back when she returned to St. Louis.

This time since Miss Trudi was with the girls, there was no need for her brothers to drive with them. Big Momma lived a sheltered life and had never seen anyone like Miss Trudi; she did not know quite what to make of her.

My mother said when they told her Miss Trudi was really a man, she thought they were teasing her and never believed it. She knew that she was big and tall for a woman, but she did not believe that she was a man under all of that hair and makeup "no way!"

It was a nice visit. Aunt Bee was her old self again, pretty, funny and happy. When it was time to leave, they all said goodbye and drove off in the new car that Papa had gotten for her. Like any father who loved his daughter, he wanted her to be safe.

Papa agreed with Bee that he would get the money back from her later. Papa had no plans to take money from Bee. He was so proud of her, and happy that she could make it on her own, but he had to do something to feel that she still needed him. He would tell her later, but for now, he allowed her to consider the money a loan.

They promised to be home for Christmas. Because of the likelihood of snow, they were going to take the train. The plan was set, even Miss Trudi was going to come back with them. She wanted to experience an old fashion country Christmas!

With each of them taking turns driving, and Miss Trudi takes the last shift, they made it back home in record time. They were all so very tired from the drive and partying while in Madisonville; they decided to go right to bed. The next day was a workday and they needed to rest.

Miss Trudi stayed over at the apartment; no one wanted to move until they had to. Bee was feeling optimistic about her future again, life *was* good!

When Aunt Bee got to work the next day, she had a letter from Bradley on her workstation, along with a dozen wilted roses. Miss Trudi asked her what was in the note, Bee said he wanted to see her that "he missed her and he wanted to apologize about the way he treated her."

"He didn't care what his family or anyone else said about their relationship, he loved her, and wanted to marry her, they could move to California, where people were more liberal."

Trudi told her to tear up the note and burn it. "A leopard does not change his spots honey. He is just angry because you broke up with him first!" Dolly's aunt agreed that she should just avoid him until he forgot about her, and moved on to someone else. Aunt Bee was not going to argue with them, life had been good since her break up with Brad.
She was happy again, having fun again; she did not want to get back into that situation. She had no desire to go back to being afraid and ashamed.

She didn't want to go back to having to lie to her friends and making up stories about why she was distant, and staying away from friends and family. Because she had to, so that she could hide the bruises, cuts and other injuries she received during her fights with Brad.

She did not want to go back to the time when she had to lie, to give the bruises time to heal. She was done with all of that. She agreed with her friends, she was going to ignore him, and stay away from him until he forgot about her, (*she hoped he would forget about her)!* After all, he *was* handsome and rich, and there were lots of girls who wanted to be with him. She prayed that he would soon forget about her, and move on to someone else, as Dolly's aunt had predicted!

⌘

Without her knowing it, Bradley had been watching Bee since the day after she told him she was moving on. He would hide across the street from the shop watching them come and go. When saw that she moved and did not call to tell him where she was going, he was furious. Brad thought to himself, "Who did she think she was?"

"She was lucky he gave her the time of day, she was just a simple Negro girl, who was **she** to avoid **him**! How dare the old woman who owned that beauty shop not allow him into her place of business- how dare they all treat *him* like he didn't matter!" The trip Bee took to Mississippi threw him off, because he was watching the shop and she had not been there in days, he was beginning to think that she had gone back to Mississippi to live. But, when he took the flowers to her, one of the ladies told him that she was due back in a day or two that she had gone to visit her family.

October 17th, 1948, after her visit home, Aunt Bee had a job with one of her white clients. The daughter of one of her lady's was getting married. It was to be a grand affair at a *big and fancy* "white only" hotel uptown.

Bee and Trudi were working on the wedding together. Because the job was so big, they hired another girl to help them. Bee knew this was the chance that she had been waiting for. This was her opportunity to really show this town, what she could do.

Bee and Trudi worked for weeks preparing, looking at the wedding colors, and dresses of the bridal party, so they could come up with ideas for each bridesmaid, as well as the bride and maid of honor. She was not going to leave anything to chance, it had to be perfect.

They hoped this was the start of something big for them; she and Trudi could start a business doing large affairs, exclusively for "white" uptown clients. They were thrilled at the prospect. Miss Trudi had not dared to even consider her career taking this direction, she was also excited. The hotel where the wedding was to be held was as elegant as it was grand! It boasted marble floors, crystal chandeliers and a beautiful garden area, perfect for a wedding.

Because it was fall, and a bit chilly outside, the wedding was indoors, inside one of the large ballrooms. But the reception was in the enclosed garden room; this room allowed the guest the option to go outside to enjoy the garden, if the weather permitted.

The air was festive and filled with excitement and promise; although they had to stay in the hotel rooms, and could not walk about the hotel alone, Trudi and Bee were having a good time.

The lady who hired them had a room for them to sleep in off of the bridal suite, in case the bride, the mothers of the bride and groom, or someone in the bridal party required a touch up. The party was to go on into the wee hours of the morning, so they had to stay over.

Although the room they stayed in was the equivalent of servant's quarters, it was spacious and clean (and the only way they could spend the night in the hotel)!

Still, it was exciting! These were the times they lived in- they didn't feel slighted by the attitude of the hotel management, after all, Trudi and Bee both knew that they weren't servants, they were providing a service as business owners, and they were being paid well for their talents.

The mother of the bride ordered food for them; everyone was in such a festive mood, she even gave them a bottle of champagne of their own to enjoy. *(**They could not drink from the same bottle as the white ladies, it wouldn't be proper**)!* Bee and Trudi were just fine with that.

This was the life she always dreamed of living. And they were enjoying every experience.

It was a long night. By the end of the reception party, they were exhausted.

Finally, the bride and groom went to their suite and she and Trudi could finally crawl into bed. Bee went to sleep feeling happy. The wedding went off without a hitch; their work was a big hit with the other female guests. They received several job offers before the affair was over. Two of the jobs were weddings! Their new business was well under way!

But before they could make plans for future work, they had to complete this job. They were up early the next morning, breakfast in their part of the suite, and then dressed the bride for her honeymoon trip.

Hair, makeup and clothing accessories, finally they were done, time to pack up to leave.

Miss Trudi volunteered to finish up getting their things together, while Aunt Bee went to pull the car around to the back of the servant's entrance.

The bride's and groom's families were rich and important people in the city, and the hotel was willing to bend a lot of rules to accommodate the wedding preparation; however, Miss Trudi walking around the hotel by herself was not something the management was unwilling to look the other way about. Trudi was not bothered by it, she told Aunt Bee "I have been thrown out of better places than this, and denied entry into worse; it's just the way of the world."

Aunt Bee laughs, grabbed as much as she could carry on her own, and went to retrieve the car. It was the servant's entrance so it was not meant to be convenient; there was no parking close to the door, so Bee had to walk quite a distance in order to reach her car. When she went outside, she heard a man's voice; he asked her if she needed help with her load.

Her first reaction was to refuse, she did not want to draw attention to herself, and she could tell by the sound of his voice that he was white. Another problem, she could do without. She was going to say thank you, but decline his offer to help.

When she looked around to thank the gentleman, who did she see standing there but Bradley!

She was almost relieved that it was him because she did not want to cause trouble by talking to a strange white-man, in the alley of a hotel, but then the look on his face made her pause. She noticed that he looked ill. He had lost quite a lot of weight, and he needed a shave. If she did not know him as she did, Bee would have thought he was a bum.

And there was something else about his posture that she could not put her finger on, but everything in her was telling her to run, to get in the car and just drive; but she could not move, something about the way his eyes met hers paralyzed her. She tried to laugh and make it sound casual, but all she could hear was her squeak out a weak imitation of a laugh.

She thought that making small talk would help her to understand what he wanted, and she hoped that he would just walk away, or that someone would come out of the hotel and give her the chance to get away from him, *in case he tried to harm her*. She knew that likely, only another servant would assist a Negro woman against a white man, even if he did look like a bum. Bee didn't care who it was; she would take what help she could get. She asked him how he had been and thanked him for the flowers. His reply was, "Look at me "Bumble Bee, *(his nickname for her)*, how do I look to you?

I have not been able to sleep since you left me, I can't eat, and I can't work."

"What happened to us? I loved you, I wanted to make you my wife, and you simply left me! You walked out, with no discussion, and not one word of warning to me; I didn't know you were going to leave. You had no thought or concern about how this would affect me!"

"I opposed my family for you, and my friends, they all said that I was a fool to waste my time on a Negro woman; but I told them that you were different, that you were special. Then you left, without a real explanation. You have to know I love you! Why did you do it? You say it was because of your family- but what is the real reason?"

"I tried contacting you time and again, you didn't respond to my messages; you moved and didn't tell me where you were going! That old woman where you work wouldn't tell me where you were. Why all the secrecy, is there another man?" **{*Isn't it amazing how someone can treat you like the dirt under the bottom of their shoe, and be completely oblivious as to why you no longer want to be around them when you leave}?!***

Now Bee was thinking fast, what could she possibly say to him that would not make him angry? Her hands were full, and he was in the way of the door, she could not go back into the hotel. She had to talk to him and try to keep him calm; she had seen him angry and it was not where she wanted him to go right now. All along, she was praying that someone, anyone would come out of that damn door!

To buy time she told him about her trip home, and that the apartment was Dolly's idea, so that she could be closer to the school. That was a lie, but she was saying anything to keep him *just* talking until someone came outside, or until he got bored talking with her, and would go away. *(Please God let him get bored and want to move on)!*

But it was not working; nothing she said made it sound like she was missing him, as much as he was obviously missing her. Although she was down playing everything she had done in the weeks since their breakup, it sounded exactly like what it was that she had moved on.

Her arms were starting to ache from holding the suitcase of makeup and hair preparation items. She wanted to put it down, but she was afraid to move.

He must have seen that she was uncomfortable, but he didn't make any moves to take the bags away from her, or allow her to go to the car. He just kept asking her why she hadn't tried to contact him.

Then he changed his posture completely, he said to her, "it's okay baby, I know that you were worried about your parents and what your brothers would think."

Bee was thinking fast, her instincts told her if she kept him talking, she could buy some more time, and give Trudi a chance to come looking for her.

Bee told him that she did not want his family to disown him for marrying a Negro; she said that she was thinking about him and his future, and how hard it would be for him if he married her.

She couldn't ask him to give up his family, and she loved her family too much to give them up, so she thought it best if they go their own way.

That seemed to cause him to ease up; his face was not as tight and angry. Bee thought this would be a good time to get the hell out of there. She told him the cases were getting heavy and that she needed to put them in the car.

That 'Trudi and the Mrs., they had been working for were looking for her to return, and she could not keep her waiting. Although part of that too was a lie, she hoped that if he knew her white employer was waiting for her, he would allow her to leave. What happened next was not at all what she expected to see him do, he started to laugh.

She didn't know if she should laugh with him or run because he had finally snapped, but still she was frozen. All she could do was stare at him; Bee thought to try to reason with him, she told him again that she had to leave.

He said to her, "You don't have to worry about the lady that you are working for getting angry, because you are finished with all that career, business, (that), as my wife you won't need to work, so just come with me and we will go on to California and get married." She could see that he was not going to be reasonable, and make getting away from him easy.

Still, she was thinking fast, she told him that she needed to collect her money for the job she had just done. He said again, "you don't need to worry about that, I will take care of you."

Then, she tried telling him that she had to pay Trudi, she had worked all night and deserved to be paid, and she was her ride home, she couldn't just leave her there! "We will take care of Trudi once we are in California, he said, we will send her the money you feel you owe her for working, but for now Trudi can take a taxi home;" *because he wanted Bee to get into his car and go with him right now!*

She knew for sure that he was out of his mind now, because he grew up in this town, and he knew that in this hotel, and in this neighborhood, Trudi would never get a taxi; she couldn't even get on the bus in this part of town safely, being who she was. Bee thought the only thing to do was to tell him she was leaving and that she was not going to marry him.

She was sorry that things didn't work out between them, but nothing was going to change, they were not going to be together. Before he could respond to what she said, she turned quickly to walk towards the car, but she didn't get three feet away before he was on her, grabbing her.

She dropped everything she was holding when he grabbed her by her hair. He pulled her head back by her hair until she was looking at him. She didn't recognize this man; in all of the times that she had seen him angry, even during the worst of the beatings, she had not seen this side of him. She never would believe he was capable of this kind of violence.

She started to scream, at this point more from fear than from pain. When she continued to scream he slapped her, he hit her so hard it knocked her "ear bobs" off, and busted her lip. She looks down and saw that she was bleeding.

This was it for her; there was no way that she was going through this again. She had been honest with him, the relationship was over, and she did not owe him anything. After all, it was he who was behaving badly. She had nothing to feel bad about, or sorry about. She was done!

Bee decided to fight back, as she had seen her mother do on too many occasions to count. She went after him with all the strength she could gather, and succeeded in scratching him across his face, and ripping his jacket and shirt.

Bee realized that she would be no match for him in physical strength, but if she went down, she planned to go down fighting! She thought this would either make him stop and leave her alone, or hit her harder; she was right about the latter. Her fighting back took him by surprise.

She saw this as an opportunity to get away from him-she tried to run, but before she could get very far, he recovered and came after her.

He caught up to her before she made it to the door of the hotel, and grabbed her. He put his hands around her neck and began to choke her; *the same hands that he once held her with-the same hands that he used to stroked her hair with when they were a couple-the same hands!*

This was not the man she fell in love with, and thought the world of at one time. Today she was praying for someone, anyone, to come out to save her from him, but no one did! She could not breathe; she was light headed from the lack of oxygen. Bee was out of breath from Brad choking her, and almost blacked-out.

She hoped he was done with her and would go away. She prayed that he had made his point and he would leave her alone! Now that she was weak and limp, and could no longer fight with him--he dragged her by her hair and the collar of her dress back to the middle of the alley, further away from the door. Then he picked her up by her collar, and began to slap her. He started to hit her; he began to beat her with his fist.

He hit her with a savagery she had never experienced before, in a way he had never beaten her before!

It was as if he was *trying* to beat her to death. The pain was so awful; he was hitting her in the head with his fist, and holding her so that she could not get away from him! When she fell to the ground because she could no longer stand, even with him holding her, he started to kick her in the head and stomp on her, in her stomach, her chest, her lower abdomen.

It was as if he was not the same man and she was not the same woman that not 10 minutes earlier, he asked to marry him! Did he not recognize her, didn't he know that she was the same woman that he said he loved, and could not live without? Couldn't he see that it was her, Bertha Sue?

Finally, when she could not take the pain any longer, she gave in to the release of the darkness, she could still feel the pain from the blows, but now she was numb. It was not as bad as it was before the darkness came.

She thought she was going to die, and she was ready to die, anything to make the pain in her head and belly go away. She was ready to give in to the peace of the darkness.

Bee did not remember what happened after that, she woke up in the hospital with Trudi and Dolly standing over her. She tried to ask them what happened, if she was in an accident. Then she remembered Brad, and the way he beat her in the alley of that "white only" hotel.

She looked around for him, she was afraid that he would come back to get her, and this time she would die, she knew it; if he came back! She tried and tried to speak, but she could not. Trudi and Dolly were both crying, and they were not looking at her. "Why were they crying, she thought, she was okay, wasn't she; for some reason she just could not talk right now."

She wanted to ask them where he was, was he locked up? Did they make sure that he could not come into her room and get her again?

She was really afraid of him this time, oddly, she had not been truly afraid of him before, because she never thought he would really hurt her. But now she was afraid, very afraid!

Then she saw her parents, Big Momma and Papa, her brothers were there, my mother, Sara was there, and her sister Ella. How long had it been? It seemed like it all happened just hours ago. All the women were crying and the men were fussing! "Someone please look at me and tell me what is going on. I am trying to speak, it is like I am opening my mouth, but nothing is coming out!"

⌘

October 20, 1948, Bertha Sue King died due to massive head trauma, she was 26 years old. My family told me that Big Momma was inconsolable, and so was Papa.

They say that Bradley must have left town right after he beat up Aunt Bee; likely, he thought the woman he loved was dead when he walked away from her, where he left her while she was unconscious on the ground in the alley!

Miss Trudi was the one who found her, yes, she was wondering what was taking her so long to get the car, so she went out to look for her, and found her lying on the ground.

Because she was in a white part of town, it took too long for the ambulance to come to pick up a Negro. It took even longer to drive to the closest hospital because they turned her away, so the ambulance had to drive to the outskirts of town to the Negro hospital.

Although Bee died days later of head trauma, her heart stopped twice in the ambulance; I suppose the ambulance doctors felt sorry for her, when you looked at her, she was so badly beaten she was unrecognizable. Her face, lips and eyes were swollen to almost twice the normal size.

They worked hard to get her heart beating again; they were really trying to save her life. "Blood was everywhere! We thought that she had been stabbed, said Miss Trudi. There was so much blood. What type of man can do this to a woman with his bare hands?" Miss Trudi swore to become Mr. Tony again, "Long enough to find his ass and beat him bloody!"

Bradley disappeared after he left the alley that night. My Mother thought that his family sent him away. Although not much was likely to happen to him for killing a black woman, it would have tarnished his family name; after all, it was murder!

Papa sent Sara, Ella and Big Momma home with Uncle Anderson on the train, loaded down with suitcases full of Bee's personal belongings from her apartment.

Papa said that he, William and his brothers from Little Rock would follow with the larger items in her car and the truck they drove to St. Louis when they receive word from Dolly that Bee had been hurt.

Young, beautiful and talented, my Aunt Bee was gone, all of her dreams and plans for the future gone with her. Why, because she loved a man? **Love is not supposed to kill you, right?** What could Bee have seen in Bradley's behavior at the beginning of their relationship, other than them being from different backgrounds, to alert her that this relationship would end badly, so very badly for her?

What could she see that would warn her that this was not the man she should be with; that this was not the relationship for her. How do you know? How can anyone know? How can a woman make a safe choice when choosing to date someone?

I truly miss Aunt Bee although I had never met her, just hearing my family speak of her makes me wish that she was still with us. I have seen hundreds of photos of her; she was surely beautiful, and seemed to have the whole world at her feet. I am certain that by not knowing her, I missed out on an adventure!

My mother, Big Momma and my aunts used to sit and talk about Aunt Bee, often. One night I overheard them say, that after the doctor told my family that Aunt Bee was dead, Papa, her brother and Papa's brothers from Arkansas, left the hospital and didn't come home for two days.

When they got home, they did not say a word to her; they just took a bath and went to sleep. Big Momma thought he was simply grieving. But later, Big Momma told her daughters that Papa said to her, *"We killed that white boy and threw him in the Mississippi River!"*

She said that she did not believe him, that she could not believe him! When he said this to her he had been drinking, and she thought it was the drunken ranting of a man who just buried his baby girl.

She said she asked him about it later, and he denied saying it, he forbid her from talking about it to anyone, and never spoke of it again!

Sadly, it took this tragedy to cause him to stop beating his own wife. And before Papa died, he told Big Momma the truth about her family, and her parents. That when they passed away, they died missing her, not being angry with her. She responded to him, "I know, I have always known."

For me it was more of an affirmation that men who beat their wives and girlfriends are not out of control, they know exactly what they are doing, even if they are extremely angry.

They are making a choice to act this way and that most can make the choice to simply **STOP IT**, where some may need professional help to change this behavior.

"WE ARE FAMILY "

Yes, yes, my family puts the **D** in DYSFUNCTIONAL, and maybe even something deeper. And we did a lot of laughing to keep from crying. Again, it was the only life that we knew; this was simply how it was for us.

Now, let us fast forward to 1967 to **my story, and my drama**. This is my story and because I am writing it, I obviously did not die from my madness. But it could have easily gone that way. Now ladies, this is not the time to stop reading my book because it is too sad, and you want to read something that is going to make you happy. Wouldn't it be grand if this world were a place where we could be happy all of the time? *We can't all be like Pharrell Williams!*

Sisters, I am trying to help you learn from my family's bad choices. So keep reading, I promise to give you something here and there to make you chuckle at times, and nod in agreement. But what I hope to do is save your life, or the life of someone you love.

So put on your big girl panties, and suck it up, keep reading! Where was I? Right 1967 Madison high school, I was dating the captain of the basketball team and chasing after the captain of the football team, because he would not give me the time of day!"

⌘

    Because I was considered one of the cute girls, and because of who my family was, I was pretty popular at school. A part of everything and every activity; Cheerleading, Glee Club, student council, debate team, (I thought I had an opinion)!
    I was a true King daughter. By the time I came along my mother had four children and two husbands, seven children in all. But she was never married to my father, and I never knew him. Big Momma said that his name is Jacob Winters, and that he was from Charlotte, North Carolina.
    I believe part of my mother's shame was she did not know much more about him than that bit of information. Since he was not there when I was born, and they were never married, I do not carry his last name, I have Papa's last name.
    I am told that Papa wanted it that way, because my mother wanted to give me up for adoption. Since she was unmarried at the time, I would be too difficult to explain to the community. Papa said no to her giving me up, that he would not tolerate his blood going into an orphanage. As long as there was breath in his body, it would never happen.
    He told her it didn't matter what she said about this, I was his blood; he was going to give me his last name, and take care of me. My mother could be a participant in my upbringing --or not, but he was not going to allow her to give me away! *Thank god for Big Momma and Papa!*
    Jacob was a soldier visiting his cousins in Madisonville when he met my pretty, newly divorced mother.

He was the cousin of a friend of my Uncle William, Papa and Big Momma's oldest son, and his wife Jamie, (I didn't know my father's cousin either). Uncle William (Will, for short) was one of the first Negro police officers in Madisonville; even though he graduated from college, he started out as a patrolman, but quickly became a Sergeant, then a detective.

At the time he brought his new friend to our house, my mother was desperate to leave Madisonville, *(running from her past instead of learning from it)*; she wanted to make a new life, away from this town and the people that knew her secrets. I supposed that life here was not very exciting for her.

Although she was educated, as were all of Papa's children, my mother never had an actual career, or a life outside of our small community. Her entire adult life she worked in my grandfather's office, keeping his books and making job appointments. Outside of the family, she did not have many activities; unlike Aunt Bee, she did not know how to escape her life in this small town.

By now Papa had twenty-four trucks for his business and a full staff of painters, thirty in all, along with a receptionist, a human resources manager, warehouse workers to manage all the materials that were used on jobs, and a sales representative who secured the contracts for the company.

In addition to managing the staff and front office, it was my mother's job to give out the work assignments to the painters; often she had to follow them to a job to collect the money, because back then, many customers paid in cash.

Most of the white customers had accounts and paid monthly. It was her responsibility to keep it all in order.

Since my father was a friend of a friend, my family did not know that much about him. The friend who brought him to dinner managed to disappear after my mother announced that she was pregnant with me. No doubt, he knew my grandfather's reputation -- I am sure that he did not want to *face the wrath of William King Sr.,* so he left town also. Likely, he feared retaliation for bringing this shame to William King's daughter, *(she did have a say in this)*!

Along with Jacob's cousin went any hope of me ever finding my father, or having any relationship with him.

I have to believe that his cousin told him about me, even if my mother did not. I never tried to look for him, because he knew where we were, and as far as I know, he never once tried to reach out to me, so I moved on also.

Papa filled the role just fine for me. I have no shame or regrets, although it took me a while to get to the place where I grew comfortable with the circumstance of my birth- the truth is that I had no control over this situation, it was my mother's cross to bear, and I have to say, she didn't handle this that well!

Uncle Will was very angry with my father, he said, his behavior was weak and spineless, that he better keep running if he knew what was good for him! That it was irresponsible to take advantage of someone's hospitality, rerun the host daughter, then leave town, *(again, she had a choice in this)!*

As Papa got older and sicker, Uncle Will moved into the role as head of the family. Uncle Will and Aunt Jamie had a small house just outside of town where most of the middle class lived. Yes, I said middle class. It is the 1950s, and Negros are now allowed to be part of middle class America.

Nice houses, nice cars, a new way of living for Black people in Mississippi. Papa said, "The war had changed things"- *but not that much.*

White police officers were still arresting and stringing up young black men for infractions as small as looking in the direction of a White woman or girl, and although my grandfather was an important man in this town, he was still a black man, and his reach could only go so far to protect us.

So as a rule, we stuck to our own neighborhoods, schools, stores, restaurants and nightclubs, it was simpler and safer! After dinner that fateful night, they all went out to a nightclub in town, my mother and father, my aunts and their husbands and boyfriends, and my uncles and their wives.

While they were all out having a good time, someone thought to take one of those black and white photos that everyone has in a frame in their house, with family and friends sitting at a table with a host of different glasses and bottles on the table in front of them.

That is the only photograph I have of my father. He left Madisonville promising to return to marry my mother. The story goes, that one of my mother's *"good friends,"* female of course, said something to my father about my mother and her habits that caused him to leave Madisonville, and not look back.

I always wondered that if he loved her, why, would he listen to a stranger and not come back for your child. That is, if he even knew about me.

These were questions I would ask my mother about my father. She would answer by yelling at me that "He was no damn good, like most men, they only want one thing, and then they leave you when they get it!
You better watch yourself Miss fast ass, or you are going to be just like him when you grow up!"

Of course, at ten, eleven and twelve years old, I had no idea what she meant when she said that I would be just like him. In what way could I do that?

I never got those answers, by this point in the conversation, depending on the time of day, it was either time for me to go to bed, or time to go to Big Momma's house and see what she had for me to do.

I think the humiliation of him leaving her caused my mother to treat me *differently* than she did my siblings. Not mean exactly, but distant.

I am certain that Papa putting his foot down about her giving me away did not help her attitude toward me and her situation. I believe that any insecurity that I would develop along with other normal adolescent issues was compounded by this lack of relationship with my mother.

But there was Big Momma; although no one ever said it out loud, I think she spent so much time with me because she knew how my mother felt about me. That every time she looked at me she would see my father, and be reminded all over again of what happened to her.

If the town was gossiping about her having a child out of wedlock, I never heard it, nor was I treated differently in the community because I was illegitimate.

Although I was not the only child in the town born of an *absent father*, I believe my mother just felt betrayed, and could not get past that feeling.

It was my job to go to my grandparents' house after school to see if Big Momma needed anything; she and Papa were older and could not do as much on their own. I would run errands, read her mail, pay her bills and take them to the post office for her.

⌘

As a pre-teen, I was either walking or riding a bike to her house to run her errands. But by the time I was ready to graduate from high school, Papa bought me a red mustang convertible! The purchase was made through my Uncle Anderson, because my mother thought I was already too fast, and "all I needed was a car to get my fast-tail in trouble."

Papa was old, but still in charge of his family, so in spite of my mother's protest, he bought the car for me anyway. I was a good student and he knew it. I was accepted into every college I applied to. But I chose to go to school close to home-- Rust College in Mississippi.

I wanted to stay close to Big Momma; I felt that she needed me. It was during the times that I was at her house running errands, and helping her with her chores, that she would teach me to cook and bake. Sometimes my sister Diane would also be there, but she was not as interested in learning to cook as I was. I never wanted to admit it to anyone, nor was I ready, or willing to admit it to myself, but I wanted to be perfect so that my mother would be proud of me.

I did everything I could to show her that I was *not going to be no good like my father*.

I tried to make her see **me**, by getting good grades, receiving lots of honors at school, and trying to always be helpful. In addition to helping my grandparents each day, I would work in the office of King's Decorating during the summer, or at the general store to help out behind the counter. The King family also owned the grocery store that was in the black area of town.

Papa's brother ran the store; he moved to Madisonville after Aunt Bee was murdered. I supposed he thought Papa needed family around during such a difficult time in his life. I also believe that he wanted to be near him, in the event that there was ever any fall out from what they did to Bradley.

Big Momma would say that being smart and being a good housekeeper along with the ability to prepare a good home cooked meal, was the only way to keep a man truly happy! She encouraged me to do well in school and learn to manage a household.

She said, "A person can never learn too much. Learn as much as you can about everything you can."(I think deep down she didn't want me to ever need to wonder, *what if...*) My job was twofold: make my momma proud, and find a good man- that's where my life plan began and ended. After all, what else was as important as marriage and family, (*I had a lot to learn about life*). With what I learned from Big Momma, I was sure that I was well on my way to having *what I wanted* out of life.

During this time in high school, the boy I was dating was the captain of the basketball team, and my future husband, Raymond Willis. Raymond was handsome and also from a "strong southern family."

Raymond's father and grandfather like my grandfather were prominent black men in the community.
Everyone expected us to get married and we both also thought that it was *the natural progression of things.*

However, all the while I was planning to marry Raymond, I was secretly chasing after Jimmy Dent, the captain of the football team, and not so secretly, Raymond was doing a bit of chasing of his own!

His reasoning was that we were going to get married anyway, so he needed to get all the *running* out of his system before the marriage, so that he would be a good husband.

If that mess didn't sound crazy to me then, it surely does now, but since I was still a virgin and had no plans to change that until AFTER our wedding. I put up with his behavior, *(better her than me right now)!*

And of course, his *messing* gave me the opportunity to do my own dirt; why let him have all the fun? I convinced myself that this nonsense made perfect sense to me.

Not knowing that this was the beginning of what was going to be a very unhealthy marriage, downhill from the start marriage. Raymond came from another founding family in Madisonville; his grandfather was in town before my grandparents moved here and started his family business in 1911. Their family business was dead people! Raymond's father was the mortician for the Negro community.

There was certainly good money in dying, because they were even better off than my family financially.

Papa and Big Momma were excited for me to make such a great match. As pathetic as it might sound, other than a host of great recipes, pitifully tucked away in my hope chest, I had no idea what it meant to be a good wife.

I could cook, and clean, and run a house with the precision of a Drill Sergeant. And I truly thought I knew how to be sexy. What a sad, sad, sight I must have been, I actually did not have a clue. I was not prepared for this chapter in my life. Being a wife and someday a mother. I did not know that it took grooming for that job as well.

I was learning by example, my family's example, and it was not always the best classroom. The saving grace for me was that in some areas of my life, I exercised my own mind.

I did not rely *on what I was told to do,* or everything I saw before me to determine how I would plan for my future. In spite of my "fastness" and my mother's predictions of my inevitable failure, I was a "good girl."

Like many of the kids, I was not *experimenting* with sex in high school. I learned about sex from movies and reading romance novels. My friends and I watched that movie, with Sandra Dee and Troy Donahue about a thousand times, you know the one; *where she gets pregnant and has a baby that her stepmother and his father raise as their own because nice white girls didn't have babies out of wedlock!*

In my naive mind, this told me everything I needed to know about being sexy. I thought with that little bit of insight, I was ready for marriage!

There was something else that I did not know about, respect in a relationship, giving it or receiving it. I was immature and selfish and didn't know it; another valuable lesson that I missed out on, but would learn later, the hard way!

I was too lazy to step outside my comfort zone and take a look at the real world. It was simpler to believe that my family name and my good looks would get me through!

I am Peaches King after all, I was sure that all I had to do was to *simply show up*, and my man would be wildly happy to have me! Part of growing was learning from experience, and I had a lot of growing to do.

I really did believe that everything that Big Momma taught me about cooking and keeping a house was all I would need to be a good wife. After all, what else is there?

I was taught nothing about compromise or sacrifice for the person you love. At the time I did not realize there was such a thing. My future husband was not much better, his family spoiled him as well; he was selfish and self-centered, and often, he was unkind.

Sometimes I would see him do and say things to other people, that I thought was down- right mean and nasty, and usually to someone who had a lot less than we did. I would look at him and could not help but to think;

He was a boy from a prominent family in our community, wasn't it his job to lead by example?

When I would question him about his bad behavior, he would laugh at me and say, "Don't be so serious baby, we young." We have all of our lives to be responsible, don't you worry your pretty head about that stuff- I will take care of you, and right now, I'm trying to protect you!"

"I will deal with difficult people or any problem so you will not have too, that is what a man is supposed to do, run interference for his woman!"

(What did that have to do with him acting like a spoiled brat)!

But because he was my future husband, *it was not my place to correct him.* I let it go; this will be the first of many times I made that mistake!

Both of us, Raymond and I cheated on each other in college before we were married, *and discussed it*! We thought we were being honest and mature!

I managed to maintain my virginity through it all, while I attended a local state university. Raymond, however, managed to father a child when he was away at school in Washington DC. He attended Howard University.

Because of what happened to my mother, I thought he was going to leave me too, just walk out because life, *(not his behavior)* had disappointed him. That life had the nerve to change his plan for the future! But he was saved by his family's wealth, and never had to be responsible for his actions, *(again)!*

Since we had not had sex, there would not be the same type of shame that my mother suffered. But I would be shamed none-the less!

Is the question in your mind, why was she ashamed? He was the one having unprotected sex and making babies with one woman, when he was committed to another!

I was not smart enough to know that **I** had been disrespected and betrayed. My **only** concern was that he had a baby with another woman, and **I** was going to be forced to live with that for the rest of my life!

I decided to get even; I planned to make his life as miserable **as mine** was sure to be because of the child. I was determined that he would pay for this betrayal forever!

In spite of these challenges, and the fact that there was a voice in my head telling me to *"run, this is not what I really wanted,"* we managed to make it to our wedding day.

June 15th, 1979. There we were, Raymond and I, the guests of honor at the biggest wedding this town has seen in twenty years, six bridesmaids, (including my college roommate) three flower girls, and my sister Diane as my maid of honor. Raymond's family provided the limousines.

It was a grand affair. Our honeymoon was in Florida, courtesy of Raymond's parents. For my wedding night, I put on my best Sandra Dee pout, (from the movie) and tried to look as sexy as I didn't feel.

Big Momma tried to tell me about what to "expect" on my wedding night as best she could, without acting embarrassed. I could tell that she was not comfortable with the subject matter, but it was important for her to be there for me, in spite of her obvious discomfort.

I could have saved her the trouble of being embarrassed. Although she knew I was still a virgin, but little did she know, that during my four years of high school, reading romance novels taught me things about having sex that I could manage to repeat **verbally**, *but I couldn't quite visualize; how could they do* **that?! (Standing up or lying down)!!**

Also, because my roommates in college knew less about sex and the male anatomy than I did-four more years of all the porn that I was forced to watch, made certain things about intercourse that I could not *visualize* from the novels, **quite clear**. But still I was clueless -watching and reading was nothing like doing! I was feisty in the streets, but I was too chicken to go fooling around with sex. I had never allowed any boy to get past first base, not even in college.

I had plans for my future, big plans, and a child out of wedlock was not part of that plan. I was my mother's daughter, **but I** learned from her mistake!

When Raymond and I finally did get around to consummating our marriage, sex felt like a fight, his wrestling me and me trying to pin him, it was a hot mess! The second night he tried to talk me through it first.

Although it was better, it was not great, at this point I am thinking, *"really, this is why the nasty girls got kicked out of school" and the "good girls were sent away to camp," for this, really!"*

In addition to the challenges with intimacy, we were off to a very rocky start! We did not like the same movies; we didn't appreciate the same books or art. I have known this man most of my life and now I find that I do not know him at all! Here we were newly married, and already at odds. But I was not going to be defeated.

It was not in my nature to give up. I could do this-this marriage gig--*I am Peaches-King after all*--anyway how difficult could this marriage thing be?!

I know I can do it; I just need to focus on what Raymond says he needs most!

When we returned home from the honeymoon, we moved into an apartment that was over the funeral home office. The apartment was large, modern and completely furnished by his parents. Raymond's family owned the building where that particular office was located.

Before we moved in, the Willis brothers used the place as a bachelor pad (if you get my drift). Raymond was taking over as president of his family business, and my job, (according to my mother-in-law), was to "quietly assist him until we started to have children."

Then my job would be to "stay home and take care of the kids, and nurture the next generation of Willis heirs!"

His mother was my teacher in all matters of funeral home mistress. I learned from her to have my hair done a certain way, my fingernails had to stay a particular length, with only *muted polish colors,* my dresses came from a boutique that could "prepare suits and dresses befitting a lady of my standing in the community." Didn't your mother teach you anything about clothing or style?" My mother-in-law would say. "After all, the King Sisters were some of the best-dressed women in the community, why are you so behind?"

She may as well had come out and called me a hick, as my husband had implied on many, many occasions. The fact is, no, my mother taught me nothing about hair, makeup and what style of clothing fit me best- she thought I was fast enough, she was not going to contribute to my inevitable downfall "by assisting me in thinking that I was cute!"

Everything I have learned about being a woman came from Big Momma, who knew nothing about fashion or style.

My aunts taught me some things about the proper undergarments and the right hose to wear for my skin color in the daytime and which colors that worked best at evening affairs, but not much else.

Either I was too busy chasing boys and working on my grades, or they were too busy with their own daughters, trying to prepare them to be perfect wives and "catch a good husband." Hopefully they made this catch before they came home from college, because there were not that many wealthy men in Madisonville to go around, so my aunts were quite strategic about where they sent their daughters to college. And here I was, married to one of the few rich black men in town, and not feeling very lucky.

Yet everyone seems to want what I have, (what they thought I had), *be careful what you wish for, you might get it!*

I was so unhappy; I wanted to jump out of a window; ***(well, I was too vain for that, but you get my meaning).***

I should have been living a dream life, but it was far from it! The truth was that besides having nothing in common, other than being from the same small town, we did not really love each other. And it didn't help matters that I had not done much outside of Madisonville, my life was centered on my family, and therefore, I was not as worldly as he was.

Because of who my family was, along with how well I could host his business events and parties; thanks to Big Momma, I was an excellent cook and hostess.

And I was pretty, and educated, so he tolerated *my country ways and "backward" habits!* Please don't feel sorry for Raymond, my husband found happiness by other means, in the company of other women!

He and the men in his family chased women like it was a sport! They had that shit down to a science, (or so they thought)! I complained to Big Momma about my situation. She said, "Don't let it upset you so, that is what men do, baby just keep a clean house, and a hot meal on the stove, and make sure he keeps his *messing* in the streets, and not at your door, you will be alright."That was not what I wanted to hear.

Besides, I had no way of knowing **how to do that**-how does one direct her cheating husband on how to cheat?

So this was it, my life was to be an unhappy housewife with a husband who fooled around and who didn't like me much because I could not turn him on the way that he needed me to? So he used this as a justification to go outside of our marriage to get is freaky needs met!
I had no one to go to who could help me to figure this out.

My mother said "you should be happy you have a good man like Raymond," and "you better be grateful that he was staying with you, and not leaving you for the other women!"

My mother-in-law also thought I should be grateful, and keep my mouth shut." Successful men need to blow off steam sometimes, because they are under so much pressure trying to keep the business going!" "Stop whining, where is your dignity?" *Excuse me! Am I missing something here, did she say **my** dignity?!* She said that I should stay in my place and do my part to contribute to the family foundation and start having babies. "What is wrong with you anyway, after all it has been two years!" What **was** wrong with **me**?

Until that very moment, I did not think about the fact that I had not gotten pregnant, not even a late period.

"No wonder you aren't pregnant," my sister Diane said. "With all of the pressure you are under from Raymond's family to be perfect, it is a miracle that your hair is not falling out!"

As true as her statement might have been, my hair was the last thing on my mind. **I had** to get pregnant; **I** had to save my marriage! Like everyone in the community, when in doubt, go to Big Momma for answers.

I explained to her that Raymond and I were trying to have a baby, and after all this time, we were still not having any luck. "Could she please help me?"

After a long speech about "these things being in God's hands; and what was supposed to be will happen naturally, and that she was not a miracle worker!"

But after looking into my sad and desperate eyes, she agreed to help nature along a bit. She gave me some herbal tea to help make me fertile, but it only succeeded in making me sick. After six months of drinking nasty tea and standing on my head after bad sex with my husband; still nothing!

Now even Raymond was starting to look at me sideways because he needed a legitimate heir (I say legitimate because by now he had two more children from outside relationships)! Who was he anyway the King of England?

Being the oldest boy, his son was next in line to take over the family business or everything would go to his brother's kids. Why this was a problem, I do not know, but he was not at all happy about it. He began to change; he became mean and started to yell at me.

Nothing I did was good enough or right for him anymore. My cooking that he once loved, *(likely the only thing that he did love about me)*, suddenly was not good enough anymore. The house wasn't clean enough anymore; the parties that I hosted were not quite done to his liking anymore. Then the name-calling started.

Was all of this because I was not pregnant, because I was not a sex kitten? What was his problem?
I did not know what to do, or where to turn. He had never hit me, but every bad name, every criticism felt like a slap, and I found myself working harder than ever to please him.

But nothing worked; although he did notice that I was more humble as I tried to make everything right with him, it seemed to calm him a bit to see me scramble to meet his every need. I really did want to save my marriage.

In my mind the change in **my** behavior was working, and **if I could just get pregnant, or at least learn to be sexier our marriage would be saved!**

"IT TAKES A FOOL TO LEARN THAT LOVE DON'T LOVE NOBODY"

Marriage and family was an important part of the King family landscape- all of my sisters, but one were married, and all to hometown boys, except for my youngest sister Vanessa.

Vanessa married a young man she met at school in Atlanta. She attended Atlanta University (this school later would become Clark Atlanta University in 1988).

Her boyfriend's name was Roger Jennings.
His family was from Chicago; he was working his way through school on scholarship and work-study, working in the school cafeteria at night. They met in the library on campus. She said that he was smart and good-looking and he made her laugh; "it was love at first sight!"

Once they started to date they were together all of the time, she even went to Chicago to meet his family-we were excited for her that she met someone who made her happy.

Vanessa and Roger decided to finish school before they would get married. It seemed that they didn't get married a day too soon because exactly **seven months** after the wedding, they had a baby, Roger Jr., and little Phillip a year later.

Vanessa wanted to enjoy her career; she said that she "didn't want a house full of babies like our mother and grandmother." She begged Big Momma to give her some special tea also. This tea, however, was to have the opposite effect as the tea that I was drinking, *and that was not helping me to get pregnant.* My tea was only succeeding in keeping my weight down, which my mother-in-law saw as "a small victory in my otherwise useless existence."

Vanessa graduated from college with a teaching degree and came home to work at the Junior high school that was adjacent to Madison High.

Wells Junior High; it was named for Christopher Wells the founder of Madisonville Mississippi back in 1860.
Her husband got a job teaching there as well, thanks to my grandfather's and my father-in-law's connections in town.

Because of his affiliation with two of the most *influential* Negro families in Madisonville, very soon he had the job of principal, soon after that, the school superintendent; all this in less than five years.

Vanessa and Roger seemed happy; they had a comfortable three-bedroom house not far from where my uncles William and Anderson lived with their wives. It was still a nice middle class neighborhood.

The house that Vanessa and Roger lived in was also provided by Papa's influence.

They were not making great money as teachers, but they lived well because they did not have to pay rent. Their salaries went into their style of living, a lifestyle that was good for Black teachers in the south or a teacher anywhere else in 1980. As I said, they seemed happy.

They both loved their children and were good parents, but something was off to me about them when they were together. They did not seem to move as one!

We didn't see Vanessa much during the week, she said, because of the children and work; she was too busy to visit. For all of the women in the King family, a clean house and home cooked meals each day were a must. Besides work, housekeeping was a part of her daily routine.

Although Big Momma was in her eighties now, we still had family Sunday dinners at her house. Papa was seen these days more than heard because of the Dementia; however, King's Decorating was still thriving under the direction of Billy James and his wife Emily.

Uncle Anderson worked in the business as well, but he did not want to be in charge officially; he didn't want to be tied to the business. He preferred to spend time with his wife; they loved to take wonderful and exotic trips together.
And at least twice a year they would drive to St Louis to see their daughter and grandchildren.

He and his wife owned a big trailer they would use on driving, trips so that they could drive in comfort. They traveled all over the country in that thing.

He said, "Life was short." He wanted to enjoy living while he still could. His motivation was watching his father waste away to nothing, having worked hard all of his life, and now he could not enjoy it!

So that he could live as he pleased, he allowed Billy to have the honor of carrying the title of manager. But behind closed doors, because he was William King's son, he was the boss. Billy and his wife were both friends of the family. Billy was once in love with my Aunt Bee.

Papa was right all those years ago about his potential. He ran the business well.

In the ten years that Billy was running the company by himself, we grew a great deal. We began to offer other services; like carpentry, plumbing, carpet and tile laying.

Yes, the business was still doing well, even though Papa could not remember who we all were most of the time.
But before he lost his mind completely he made some additional changes. Uncle Williams's wife Jamie worked in the front office along with my mother.

Now it was her job to keep the books, pay the taxes, and keep payroll. *The King family still handled all of the money!* The family business was the foundation and security for the future for Papa's children, his grandchildren and hopefully their children; and right now it was solid, he had chosen the right man to keep it going.

Although Uncle Anderson did not spend a lot of time at the company, his role was crucial to our ability to function efficiently. Uncle Anderson supervised ordering equipment-- trucks, tools and such; he was teaching his son to do the same thing. Right now, his son Anderson Jr. (A.J.) was in charge of meeting with the contractors and ensuring that whatever services we were providing was done to the customer's satisfaction. A.J.'s wife Tina also worked in the company; she worked as somewhat of a sales representative.

Tina was a beautiful woman, very stylish and well spoken, *that is when she wasn't acting loopy!*

Her job was to bid on service contracts for the company. Although she acted as if she was off her rocker most of the time, she was very good at securing contracts for King's Decorating. The Legacy continued!

Life appeared to be good for everyone, however, in real life; most things are not what they appeared to be. Raymond and I were still struggling to get through our marriage day to day. His cheating was starting to get to me. I was so fed up with his behavior I was ready to explode!

Unfortunately, I was not the only King, daughter going through something, Vanessa was acting strange.
She missed a couple of our family Sunday dinners, and Big Momma's 85th birthday party.

She said that one of the boys was ill, and she had to stay home and take care of her child. When I called her that afternoon to see what was up, she told me "all was well, I am trying to get little Phillip to rest." That she would go by Big Momma and Papa's house during the week and wish her a happy birthday, and drop off her gift.

She knew it was not about a gift for Big Momma. She loved to have her family around her. Vanessa also knew how important the family coming to the house was to her.

It was not like Vanessa to miss such an important family event, but if her child was sick, I supposed that it could not be helped. I went by her house the someday as the birthday party to take her a piece of birthday cake, and check on her. Roger opened the door for me.

He said that she was trying to get their son to sleep. She was having a difficult time because their little boy was fussy, and that he had a fever. He said that he would have her to call me later. Instead of waiting for her to call me, I went to the school to see her the next day, Monday, so that I could talk with her, but she was not at work.

The school secretary said that she called in sick, not that her child was sick, but that **she** was sick. My first thought was "that heifer was pregnant again, and I still didn't have a hint or sign that I was with child. What was wrong with **me**?!" *Why was I having such a difficult time!*

Determined now to find out what was going on with her, I went back to her house the very next day.

Roger was not home-- when she opened the front door, I could not believe what I saw. My sister was black and blue; she looked like she had been in an accident, or the victim of a very hard fall! "What happened to you?" I asked her!

Looking either shocked or annoyed to see me, (likely both) she said, "I was putting away linens on the top shelf of the closet, and the chair fell from under me. I hit my head and fell on my face on the way down." Sounded a bit strange to me, but I had to believe her, because what else could it be?

In a voice that was a weak effort to sound matter of fact, she said, "I didn't want to alarm anyone in the family, because the bruises make the injuries look worse than they are, so I decided to lay low for a few days until the bruises healed. That's all, no big deal."

No big deal, "If it was not a big deal miss thang, why make up a lie about one of the children being ill?" Why not just say you couldn't make?"

Looking around her kitchen, I could see that the house was in its usual spotless state, but there was nothing cooking, or baking, very strange.

"It wasn't exactly a lie," she said, now sounding defensive, "Little Phillip did have a slight fever, and we thought it best if we stay home."

Then she looked at me with *that I got you* smirk of hers' and said, "If I said I had fallen off of a chair, and that was all, you know *our family;* you all would not simply leave it at that, case in point; your determined effort to talk with me in person; even going to my job to get answers!"

"Really Peaches, what was that about?" She had me there, trying not to sound as guilty as I was feeling, I said, "Okay, I apologize if I overstepped any boundaries;" *but my family meant the world to me, all we had was each other, weren't we obligated to look out for one another?*

"I just wanted to make sure you were okay, that's all." I was worried about you." With a half-smile, she said, "I forgive you *this time,* for getting so deep in my business. But in the future, can you let me *call you,* and tell you what's going on?"
"If I need help, I know how to ask for it!"

The excuse about falling off a chair worked that time, and I agreed to stay out of her business, *for now!*

I let it go and we moved on to other topics. But the next time an unexplained issue caused her to miss my anniversary party; we knew something more than accidents and sick babies was going on with her.

Yes, I was still married to Raymond, who was starting to get restless again, in spite of my best efforts to be the ideal wife. Lucky for me, I had a big announcement to make at the anniversary party!

After five years of trying, I was finally pregnant! Raymond was elated; I had not seen him genuinely smile at me since before we were married. *And I need Vanessa's ass to be there basking in my glory, for once!*

The next afternoon I showed up at her house, *(again unannounced),* with my sister Diane, and my brother James in tow. We knocked on the door and rang the bell, but no answer. Madisonville was a small town, although the street where my sister Vanessa lived was peppered with "educated black folk" *(as Papa would say),* but no matter how much education people might have, they can still remember how to be nosy neighbors.

Miss Molly and her old maid sister Paulette lived next door to Vanessa and Roger. They would babysit the boys sometimes on the rare occasion that Vanessa and Roger had to work late, or had a business event to attend. Otherwise, they rarely went out without the children.

So, when we did not get a response at the door, I went to their house to see if they knew where my sister was.

Miss Molly came to the door when we rang the bell; she said that she had the boys with her because Vanessa and Roger went to the hospital-- Vanessa had fallen off a chair again, this time putting dishes away.

I asked her why she had not tried to contact any of us. I was positive Vanessa had given her phone numbers to call in case of emergencies.

She said that was going to be her first step, but Roger stopped her. He told her not to alarm Vanessa's family, because it was a simple fall, and we Kings had the bad habit of blowing things out of proportion.
"Everything would be fine, that he would take care of Vanessa." Is that a fact! We rushed to the hospital and called the rest of the family before leaving Miss Molly's house.

When we got there, Roger was in the waiting room looking ill himself. When Uncle William asked him what happened at the house, he could not look him in the eye.
 He just kept looking down, and looking guilty, saying that she had fallen, and when he tried to catch her, she fell on top him, which is why he had a scratch on his forehead and cheek.

Sounded fishy to me, but my uncles, cousin and brother appeared to think all was well. When the nurse brought her out she looked a bit worn, but she *appeared* to be okay. She had a big red mark over her eye and her lip was busted, but other than that, she just looked very tired.

As soon as Vanessa was released from the hospital, her sisters wanted to take her home. It was late, and we were all exhausted. We wanted to get her children from Miss Molly, not that we were worried about the boys; we knew they were in good hands.

But we wanted to put them to bed, and find out from **Vanessa**, what the hell happened at her house! What was she not telling us?

All of the accident stuff could not be normal. Luckily, we knew the boys were okay and had not been hurt. We were certain that the two spinsters, who were also retired school teachers, would feed the boys, bathe them, as well as help them with their homework if they had any.

And we were right. When we got to the house, both boys were bathed; they were fed and ready for bed.

My uncles, brother and cousin opted to take Roger for a drink to "calm his nerves;" because my cousin A.J. said, "He looks like he could use a drink!"

After we got her home and the boys were settled in their beds, Diane made us all a cup of tea. As the rest of us danced around the big question, my mother came out and asked Vanessa "if all of this was really about accidents, or if Roger had hit her?" I was not sure if she was going to tell the truth, or if she would give us one of those philosophical answers she was known for; it was her way of avoiding any uncomfortable questions. Vanessa could not look at her, she seemed very uncomfortable.

She did a lot of squirming and moving around, but finally she said that he had in fact hit her. In a calm way that was out of character for my mother, she then asked her "if it was the first time, "Vanessa said no, that it happened before."

Then, with more anger than *I thought*, she should be directing **at us**, she said, "This was all the fault of the family," her husband resented us for always being in their business. "There was always a King family function that demanded mandatory attendance, and they could not have a life of their own!"

"My uncles and other men in our family made him feel like less than and man, because he wasn't from Madisonville and he wasn't a King! — And that "we thought we were so much because we had money, when in fact we were all just a bunch of country hicks!"

I could not believe my ears! Was I hearing this right? Was she actually blaming this shit on us?! And did he have the audacity to call **us** names! She was trippin!

"We might have been hicks, but we are rich hicks, and he was living quite well off of our hick money!"

I couldn't wait to see that fool. How dare he hit my sister, and then complain about all of the help our family is giving his sorry ass! Of course, the family was divided about how to address this issue.

Because of the way they were raised, Big Momma and my aunts' told her to "just try and be a better wife, maybe have another baby," *(was that the answer to all marriage issues).* And for her to try and "be more of a help to her husband" — while her sisters wanted to take him outside and beat the hell out of him!

My mother was steaming mad, she was not saying much, but the look on her face said it all, she was fuming. I was curious to see how she would advise my sister on how to handle this issue in her marriage, because she consistently encouraged *me* to stay and take the shit *my* husband was dishing out! I know I wasn't her favorite, but damn!

But today was not about Raymond or me, it was about Vanessa and Roger, and how we would find the strength to move on from this new dilemma. While supporting her and giving her the help she needed to get through this!

Vanessa said "Your reaction is *exactly* the reason I hadn't said anything to you all about my problems with Roger! You always want to take charge! I am an adult after all, a grown woman, with my own children; I don't need you all to fight my battles for me!"

My head was spinning; I had to take a breath. Right now, she needed our help, and I know it was not safe for her or the boys if she tried to handle this situation all by herself. We had to help her, even if she did not want our help!

I asked her why she thinks he started to hit her. She told us that this was not the beginning of the fighting. "The physical violence actually started back in college!"

They had been together for two years in school before they came home and were married. Had he been hitting her all of this time! Why didn't we know?

I was feeling as if I was on a really bad drug trip, *(What? I was a teenager in the 60s, I said I didn't experiment with sex, I said nothing about drugs*!*)*

I tried to make sense of this whole situation. How could we not see that something was wrong? They looked like the perfect family, so happy, *so normal.*

He seemed to love her and the boys. There were no outward signs that there was anything going on in their relationship that we should be concerned about. They went on family vacations together; they went to church together-- **Church!** Did he actually hit his wife; and he was a **Deacon** in the church. This was unheard of!

Of course, all of her siblings were outraged. We wanted to deal with him and this bad behavior! Remember that even though this is now 1985, there were still no laws that regulated domestic violence in this Country!

It was considered family business, and often the law did not want to get involved. Besides, who actually were we going to call? Madisonville had ninety police officers, and only ten black police officers; one of them was our uncle.

At this time, although there were no real laws governing family violence in Mississippi, the men in my family could not exact the same justice for Vanessa that they did for Aunt Bee.

This was not 1948, it was 1985. If they did go after Roger in retaliation for what he had done, perhaps they may not get the death penalty for killing a black man, but it was not going to be ignored like it was in the 1940s.

When talking about that situation and Aunt Bee's murder, Big Momma would say that the only hope for justice for a Negro in the south back then was 'COLD JUSTICE.'

My sister Vanessa insisted that we all mind our own business, "Don't you all have enough problems in your own lives and marriages? How is it that you have time to poke around in mine?!"

The idea of her being hurt distressed us all. But at that time, people had a very different idea about how to handle family violence. Often both families would allow the couples to work out their own issues. We all believed that when she got tired of the drama, the women would leave.

We did not have a name for it, but that didn't mean we were not familiar with it.

Within many families in the town there were rumors of violence; husbands killing wives, wives shooting at cheating husbands, even the occasional family fight where a dating couple would get into a physical altercation, at a picnic or event.

There have just been no guidelines to follow with cases of family violence. Lord knows there were no services to assist a woman who found herself in this situation. They always relied on family to take them in, help them move out, or handle the abuser. So no, we did not like that this was happening to our baby sister, but it was her life, what could *we* do? It was her life, her choice, right?

Vanessa was correct about her siblings having their own issues with their marriages and lives.

Allow me to introduce you to my sisters and brothers

⌘

My Mother- Sara Lynn's children
My Sisters and Brothers

Phyllis Gray -My sister, DOB-1944 –Phyllis was the oldest girl and without question, the prettiest; also without questions the wildest. She would come and go as she pleased. She had two little boys and a little girl all by different fathers. Phyllis barely finished high school, and didn't go to college. She drank to the point of falling down drunk, *(often my Uncle Will would have to go and get her, after she passed out in a bar or hotel lobby)*. Although she was helpless in this state, no one dared mess with her, because of who her grandfather and uncles were.

Big Momma said "Papa spoiled her, because she looked so much like Big Momma did as a girl, that she was ruined." Although Phyllis was a total mess, she would turn her nose down to us. She never had time for her younger siblings, unless she needed a sitter. For most of their lives, Big Momma and Papa raised her children, but when Papa became ill, Big Momma couldn't take care of them anymore.

So, Phyllis would just drop her children off at the house of whomever she managed to find at home. Phyllis's kids were basically nice children, so most of the time we didn't mind keeping them. We actually thought that being with her was a detriment, so in the best interest of the children, until they were older, as a family we took care of them. It wasn't their fault that their mother was a nut!

We took complete care of her kids, often clothing them, taking them to special occasions, celebrating birthdays, and school events for her. And this heifer never once thanked us. She acted as if we were supposed to take care of her children, like we were the help or something. *I am sure you guessed that we were not close!*

George Gray- My brother, DOB 1945 died 1965- my brother was so good-looking the women in Madisonville are still mourning his passing. He had a smile that would stop traffic. He was tall, athletic, and well built; he was witty in a way that didn't insult people around him.

His good looks did not spoil him, but his family did. He was sweet, but not at all responsible.

Like Phyllis, he was a bit wild, but never to hurt anyone. It seemed his life plan was just to have fun.
Big Momma said he seemed troubled, but no one ever knew what troubled him, except that he drank, a lot.

Papa wanted to teach him to take over his business, but he was nothing like Papa. He did not want to be in business, he just wanted to enjoy life. George didn't have a serious bone in his body. It was as if he knew that he would die young, perhaps he had the gift of sight like Big Momma!

He liked the girls enough, but we didn't see him settling down. He would get in that car of his and drive away. Often we would not see him again for days--- his unpredictable behavior kept our mother worrying about him all of the time. George was attentive and extremely kind to me.

I believe he felt sorry for me because everyone knows that our Mother treated me different. He would never say it, but I think that is why he always would do little things to make me happy. He would single me out to say something nice to me, or take me for a ride in his car without me asking him

. Everyone enjoyed his company because he was so much fun and easy to be around. George was partying and drinking with some friends in Jackson one weekend, when he got in his car and drove it into the side of a tree, he didn't survive the crash. It was interesting to our family that he left home with a car full of friends, but managed to be the only one in the car when it crashed!

Janet Gray-Stewart My sister-DOB 1947- also married, with one child. Her husband Damon runs the General Store in the Negro community-- (sorry this is the 80's, the Black community). Our community grocery store or general store was also a legacy of Papa. After Papa's brother retired Damon and my brother James took over the store.

If he is angry about the business being handed down to him by our family, Damon never said so, he runs the business with pride, and it has grown to have a second store in the once white's only community.

My sister Janet looks more like Papa's side of the family than the rest of us. She was shorter and darker. In her mind it caused the family to treat her differently. I do not actually believe that was true, but this perceived difference, sometimes caused her to be distant from the family.

She doted on her only son; we are not sure why they never had more children, but their life the way it was seemed to work for them. Of all of the siblings, they seemed to have the most normal marriage of Sara's children, life the way it was seemed to work for them.

I think because of her self-imposed differences, she spent most of her holidays and summers away from our family, with her father and his side of her family, and his new wife in Jackson Mississippi. She and her husband were our role models for a happy marriage.

She treated Vanessa like she was her second child. She dressed her when she was little, combed her hair and pretty much took care of her growing up, because our mother worked. I am sure that this was a big help to her. Whatever problems she and her husband might have, they kept them well hidden. No cheating or fights, just quiet living!

Diane Gray-Polk, My sister DOB, 1949- For some reason, although Vanessa was her baby, Diane was my mother's favorite, and she was the most like Big Momma in posture and attitude. Like she didn't understand the world, but she was going to make the best of it anyway. She was married, but her husband was killed in the Vietnam War.

They had two children, but she never remarried. She liked to live in the past; history was easier for her I supposed than her present life. She was a bit eccentric for a woman as young as she was.

Although pretty, she dressed and acted as if she was 30 years older. She stayed to herself, but loved her family. She is willing to be there for all things King. Although I was close to all of my sisters (but Phyllis), she and I seemed to get along together better than with the rest of the sisters.

I don't know why, but we understood each other! Actually, the family was her only social life, she didn't dance or go out, and she didn't have many friends still living in Madisonville.

When she is not out with family, she is at home with her children, sewing or watching old reruns on the television. That was her life. She was not interested in being in a relationship. She would say that "my life was just fine the way it is, I am not getting on anyone's nerves, and there is no one to get on mine!

Dora "Peaches" King, "that would be me"- DOB-1951- I was the odd man out, and as you read more of my story you will understand what I mean.

My first husband was Raymond Willis; we have one son, Raymond Jr., born in 1986 and the joy of my world!
My marriage to Raymond Sr., was volatile at best. I believe that we never really loved each other; we got married because it was expected of us.
Although from "good" southern families, we were never taught what the meaning of true love was with the opposite sex; or about respect or compromise between two committed adults.

There was no one to teach us these things, either of us. My mother and her sisters told me that my grandfather abused my grandmother for years, until a tragedy caused him to change his ways.

During those years, when he wasn't hitting her, he was cheating on her, with women all over the county.

I never knew of my husband's father ever hitting his mother, but Raymond's father cheated on her as well, and did not respect his home and family. Even on the day before their wedding, he slept with his mistress.

It was not uncommon for men in our community to have "outside" families, and they were not always well kept secrets. The wives accepted their fate. They looked the other way, never making a fuss, like the "strong southern women" they were, and made the best of a bad situation.

I tried to fall in line like the other wives in our community; be quiet and strong, as I tried to "sleep in the bed I made," *(my mother's words, not mine)*. I had no problem taking responsibility for any drama that I may have contributed to my marriage problems. But I didn't know what I should do the fix the problems we were having.

No-one said that I should have better, that I should leave my husband because of the way he treated me.

Something in my spirit screamed at me, that this was not what I deserved, that I should have better. So I left my abusive, cheating husband to make a life I could live on my own terms, *best decision I ever made!*

Vanessa Phillips-Jennings, my baby sister- DOB 1953-died 1985-Vanessa was the baby and the quietest of all of us. She studied hard and tried to follow the path I laid in high school, (the good stuff). Cheerleading, glee club, (poor thing could not carry the slightest tune) so that activity didn't last long. She was a member of the Student Council and class president.

Although Papa was going to pay for her education, she won two academic scholarships.

As a reward, he bought her a new car before she went to school. Just like with Aunt Bee, Papa wanted his girls to come home when they needed to. He was going to make it easy or her to do so. She and two friends would drive home together for most holidays. When she didn't want to drive, Papa bought her an airline ticket so that she could fly home. It was the same with his grandchildren as it was with his children. Nothing was too good or too much.

He bought the house for her and Roger when they got engaged; it was a wedding present. He wanted to help her and her new husband after Vanessa told him that Roger came from a poor family. Instead of being grateful, this fool was mad because he was getting help! Roger Sr. severely betrayed our family; the outcome was so devastating, that it almost destroyed us!

James Phillips, my Brother-DOB 1954 died 1996. James was quiet and smart like Vanessa. Today he would be called a nerd. Growing up, my mother thought, he played too much with the girls, but he was fun to have around. He worked with Janet's husband in the General store; he was the butcher, and a genuine nice guy.

He married a nice quiet and plain girl from town. This was surprising because he was as handsome as any of the men in the King family and by simply being a King he could have anyone he wanted. But he chooses Ellen Berry.

Like I said before, nice girl from another good, Southern family, but quiet like he was. They had one daughter and one son. Because they were so polite to each other I could not imagine them having sex!

But they seemed happy. Their marriage appeared to be a good one. They were content to spend time with each other; with the exception of a few King family events, they kept to themselves. They would visit equally between his family and hers. As quiet as he was, my brother had a secret. He would disappear for hours on the weekends. A couple of times he didn't come home until the next day.

Because he was a man, we surely stayed out of their business. I guess it was her family that had to deal with the issues, and whatever she was going through because of my brother's *unusual* habit.

But she and James seemed to have an understanding about it. I never saw them fight or argue. Whatever my brother was doing when he was away from home; he kept it quiet and away from his wife, and small family. I never heard her say an unkind word to or about my brother. I never once heard her complain. *How did she do it?*

If I were smart, I would have asked her how she did it. How did she look the other way when she could not account for her husband's time and his behavior?

However, I let it go, and pretended not to notice, like all of the women in our town, concerning most of the activities of their men. My brother was no exception. Sadly, my brother died of cancer of the Pancreas when he was 42 years old. I still think about him every day and miss him so much.

So there, you have it; my small section of our dysfunctional lot.

  I know that our family has problems, but we love each other in spite of our many issues. Big Momma and Papa did the best they could to make us happy in the only way they knew how. Some of our family members say that Papa never got over Aunt Bee's murder.

  Her tragic death is why he spoils his children and grandchildren, so that we would want to stay close. But no amount of love or money can keep tragedy at bay, no amount! Things pretty much went back to normal if that is what you can call *normal;* after we found out that Roger was hitting Vanessa. There had not been any "accidents" for months (*that we knew of*), between she and Roger.

  They started coming around, but only when they wanted to. No more mandatory attendance. We tried not to be hostile toward Roger Sr., but it was difficult to pretend that we all did not want to kick his ass! I wanted to believe that seeing them together was a sign that things had gotten better-that they would be okay- now the focus can **be back on me,** and I could plan for *my* baby and upcoming baby shower, and the delivery of my little bundle of joy!

  Sad to say that normal was to be short lived. The week after Christmas, Janet received a call from Miss Molly, saying the boys came running into her house out of breath, crying that someone hurt their mommy.

Janet, of course activated the King phone chain, and we all came running!

⌘

When we got to Vanessa and Roger's house my sister was lying on the floor, and she was not moving!

We couldn't see her well because the EMTs were there working on her, and preparing her for transport to the hospital. Her house was an active crime scene. The police wouldn't let us go any further into the house.

What we could see, looked as if there had been a train wreck though the kitchen! From where we were standing, we could not tell what happen to her simply by looking at her. She was lying on the floor and she was so still!

When they started to examine her we were asked to leave the house so paramedics and the police could do their jobs. We went next door to Miss Molly's as they were taking her to the hospital. We waited there for Uncle William to tell us what was going on.

While we all went to the hospital, Diane decided to take all of the children from Miss Molly's house to her house, to get them cleaned up, so that Uncle William could talk to Vanessa's boys, and try to get an understanding of what happened to their mother. But where was Roger Sr.? What happened? Did someone break into the house and hurt her?

We wanted answers. The police searched and searched the house for clues as to what happened to Vanessa.

Her oldest boy was the only witness, although he was only nine years old, he was very smart. He told Uncle William what happened as best as his nine year old mind could relate it.

It seems that Roger worked late on this day and when he came home, he was in a foul mood. Although the children were out of school for the winter holiday break, the school board members had access to the administration building.

As superintendent, Roger would often work through holidays to catch up on project deadlines or paperwork. Vanessa was bathing the boys to put them to bed.

In the time it had taken her to bathe and dress the children, his dinner had gotten cold. When he came in Vanessa asked him why he was so late. Roger Jr. recanted to Uncle Will that his father said to his mother that "she had no right to interrogate him about where he has been; because your family thinks they own this town, they didn't own him.

He didn't need to answer to her or any other King. He was tired of all of us, and tired of living in this country ass town, he was taking his boys and moving back to Chicago. Vanessa tried to ask him what brought this on.

She thought that things had gotten better. They were spending more time away from the family; only coming around when they wanted to. She thought things were going well. So what was the matter with him today?

At this point, as her little son described it, Roger Sr. hit her with the back of his hand. Although we had seen the scratch on his face that one time, we never imagined that my sister had learned to fight. I guess there was a lot about her life that we didn't know. Roger Jr., went on to tell us that his mother said to his father, "she was tired, and she didn't want to fight; she was not in the mood. She hadn't been feeling well, and would heat the food up so he could have his dinner."

"There was no need to fight about it!" When she turned to walk to the stove, he grabbed her from behind by her hair and slammed her into the refrigerator... he said "How dare you turn your back on me when I'm talking to you!" She thought she was too damn good- so high and mighty, that was her problem in the first place!

That is when he grabbed her and she began to fight him back. Roger Sr. slapped her again. This time she stood for a minute and touched her face to see if she was bleeding. When she saw the blood, she went after him again. Slapping him, scratching him, and ripping his shirt. That seemed to be the trigger he was searching for.

The young man described how his father grabbed his mother by her shirt and began to hit her in the face with his fist. She put her hands up to try and stop the blows, but he would knock them out of the way, as he hit her.

When Vanessa managed to break free by scratching at him she ran. She tried to get away from him, but he ran after her and grabbed her by the hem of her dress, and was able to drag her back. When she slipped and fell during the struggle, he sat on her. Then began to beat her about the face and body with his fist, as if he was fighting another man!

The little boy was talking very fast now, as if he was describing something that he was seeing on television. As if he was remembering it as someone else. As he was watching the horrible scene unfold, he said he heard "cracking or crunching" *he had no way of knowing that it was the sound of his mother's nose and jaw breaking!*

He said that his father just kept hitting her and hitting her. Finally, Roger Jr., tried to run up to him to hit him and get him off of his mother, but he slid on something slick on the floor and fell down. He was so distracted by what he was seeing, he didn't realize that it was his mother's blood on the floor that caused him to slip and fall.

He said that he yelled at his father to stop--but he did not stop hitting his mother. He just kept on hitting her until she stopped moving. Then Roger Jr. said that he grabbed his brother who was also watching the horrible scene, and ran with him over to Miss Molly's house.

He tried to return to his house so that he could help his mother, but Miss Molly would not let him go. When she saw the blood all over his pajamas she called the police.

Then she called us. My mother was beside herself with anger and grief. She could not believe that Roger had gone this far. She said, "It doesn't matter that Papa is in no condition to take justice because when I found Roger I am going to kill him myself!" She went from cursing to crying, back and forth. She could not control it.

We were all devastated by this horrible turn of events. We could not believe this terrible thing happened to her, and in front of the children! We waited to hear from the doctors, but I know deep down, we all knew.

Although we could not get very close to the crime scene we could see all of the blood and as still as Vanessa was, we knew she was gone, but we wanted the doctors to come back and tell us that we were wrong. That she was okay, and, she was going to make it!

⌘

    No one told Big Momma about Vanessa. We thought the shock would kill her. She was with Janet because Janet could not stand to be here at the hospital any longer, so she left to go and take care of Big Momma and Papa.

    Papa was bed ridden now. He didn't speak or respond when spoken to. It was a good thing that he would not know, that the same thing that happened to his daughter all those years ago, was now happening to his granddaughter. Murdered in the same manner, beaten to death by a man that was supposed to love her; with his bare hands! Oh, how blessed he was that he was spared that pain!

    We did not get the news from the doctors that we wished for that day. Our prayers were not answered. Tragedy struck in threes. Vanessa was dead-she was 32 years old and the mother of two young children, with one on the way. The doctor said that she was six weeks pregnant.

    We don't think Roger knew that she was with child. If he had, would he have stopped beating her?

    Although we could not tell Papa, what was happening, Janet said, for no apparent reason he started to cry! He was kept as comfortable as possible these days, because there was not much more we could do for him.

    Uncle William had a full-time nurse in the house 24 hours a day, so he could not have been suffering from physical discomfort. He suddenly started to cry for no reason that anyone could see, and then, he simply stopped breathing.

    Did he have a sense of something? Janet had not told Big Momma what happened yet, so how could he?

I never felt so much pain in all of my days. I thought when my brother George was killed, that nothing could hurt like that ever again, but this, this was far worse than I could ever put it into words. I could not catch my breath. Even Raymond was moved.

He was there for me, really there for me. And as much as I welcomed his comfort it was not enough, the shock and pain was almost too much.

I thought I would go into labor; the doctors had to give me something to calm me down. It was too soon, I was only eight months pregnant.

Please God don't take my sister, my grandfather and my child that I have waited so long for and prayed so hard for, all in the same day!

That pain we were spared. I was hyperventilating, and could not catch my breath. But Raymond had me checked into the hospital overnight to be on the safe side. I welcomed the chance to be alone with my grief, I needed to be alone.

They found Roger Sr., the next morning at his office; he had hung himself in the men's bathroom in the school district office with his belt.

The janitor found him when he went in to clean the bathroom before the business day began, because the school was still on the holiday schedule, no one saw him go into the building. I did not know a lot about Roger or his family. We had only met them a couple of times, at the wedding and when baby Phillip was born.

I do not know what happened in his life that would push him to murder his wife and then kill himself!

This was all too heartbreaking to believe, *the curse continues!* When I said that tragedy hit us in threes that day I was speaking of my sister, my grandfather and my sweet unborn niece or nephew that was murdered by his own father, before he or she even had a chance to take a breath.

Roger's death was not a tragedy to us, it was a blessing. As cold as that sounds, I didn't want one of my brothers or my uncles wasting their life going after him.

If they had found him alive, they would have killed him. There was no doubt in anyone's mind.

I didn't want him to take anything more from my family; he had taken far too much already!

We still didn't know how to tell Big Momma about Vanessa, she was 86 - still feisty, but we didn't believe that even she was strong enough to take all this on at one time. She seemed to take Papa's passing well. I supposed she knew it was a matter of time for him, likely she thought that he was suffering. I am guessing she felt his home going was a blessing and a relief. But Vanessa, not Vanessa; she had a whole life to live. How will we ever tell her?

"WHAT BECOMES OF THE BROKEN HEARTED?"

We were simultaneously planning for two funerals. Of course, Raymond's family was to handle the services.

However, because of who Papa was in Madisonville, and the magnitude of the tragedy surrounding Vanessa's, death, the white Funeral Home director from *Adam Cooper Funeral Home and Mortuary*, *(our counterparts in the all-white part of town)*, contacted Raymond and offered to handle all of the services for him personally. Roger was given over to the state; we did not care what happened to his remains.

However, we did try to contact his family, because of the good Christians that we were. But his brother wanted money to get his body back to Chicago.

They heard we had it! I had never heard my Uncle Anderson curse; I don't have to say that was not going to happen! The only way they would get his body was to come and get it, and we doubted they were going to do that, even if they did have the funds.

Roger's mother did apologize to Uncle William for what her son had done, and asked our family for his forgiveness, but that was a long way off. At this time that was far too *Christian*, even for us Southern Baptist!

Finally, we could not put if off any longer, we had to tell Big Momma about Vanessa and the baby.
But before we could say anything to her, she told us that she had a dream about Vanessa. She had come to her in a dream dressed all in white smiling and carrying a baby.

She told us Vanessa was trying to say something to her, but she could not hear what she was saying. The dream brought a strange sort of peace to her, then, "Vanessa smiled, and walked away, with the babe in her arms!"

First, she felt that Vanessa was there to comfort her about Papa's passing, but then she thought to herself, "When does the living come to you in dreams to comfort you about the dead?" She said that was how she knew when her mother and her father had passed away.

They came to her in a dream, just like Vanessa! She did not fault us for trying to keep it from her -she knew that we were trying to protect her from the pain of so much loss. She didn't ask us how Vanessa died or what happened to Roger, and we were happy to leave it at that.

On that cold day in January, we laid to rest my baby sister, and her sweet baby lying still, beside her, and our grandfather. A man who beats his own wife for years, yet we mourned his passing.

Was it wrong to mourn a man who had behaved in the same way as the other men who have cost our family so much?

I can see why loyalty in family violence can be so confusing for the families of the victims, and for the families of the abuser. On the days that he is not screaming, yelling and hurting, is he a good man?

Or because he is screaming, yelling and hurting he is not really a good man, just a man behaving badly? Where do you draw the line? Where should your loyalties be?

What would have happened to all of us, if Big Momma left Papa the first time he hit her and she had gone back to her parents in Arkansas? Where would our family be today if the tragedy of my Aunt Bee's murder had not made him see how hurtful and destructive his behavior was?

What if that event had not forced him to change his ways, before the same thing happened to Big Momma at his hand, or if one of her sons killed him in retaliation for hurting their mother? How different our lives would have been if any of those events happened a different way.

Relationship violence can change your life in a split second! And as final as abuse seems to be, there can be no do-overs! You have to make the right choice the first time around. But for Big Momma, there were no options, or choices when she was young and raising her family. It simply was the way it was.

She had to deal with it. Maybe it was her natural wisdom that saved her and Papa from the same fate as Aunt Bee and Bradley, and Vanessa and Roger.

Again, it could have been different, very different.
I wonder if she ever thinks about that when she stares out of the window and seems so far away, and "wonders what if." I will ask her the very next time I see her!

⌘

The natural thing was that Janet and her husband would take care of Vanessa's children. I don't think we ever discussed it as a family, it just seemed to happen, and we were all fine with it. She loved Vanessa so much, we all knew that with her and Damon was the best place for the boys to be.

We were taking Roger Jr., to counseling. His little mind had done too much over the past weeks, but we were not sure how to help him. He asked us, "Why did my daddy want to hurt my mommy? Didn't he love her anymore?"

He said his mother would tell him that "you should not hit or try to hurt other people, especially your family," when he was being mean or fighting with his baby brother. So why did his father behave that way toward his mother?

I surely was not the one to answer those questions about proper behavior and respect for a loved one. I was never in a position to know what was proper myself!

In spite of pain and sorrow and no matter how substantial your disappointment, life will keep moving on. Two and one half weeks after we buried my sister, I went into labor, and it was nothing pleasant!

Big Momma was there to hold my hand through the entire thing. Thank God for Big Momma!

She was my rock. I was so afraid of what was happening to me. I did not understand it, but she talked me through it, and in the end I had a beautiful baby boy.

My son, this precious life that I had brought into the world; a young man, but how can I keep him from becoming his father or grandfather?

What can I say to him to make him understand that loving someone should not cause them pain? And that being in love means that you take care of the people you care about, and not want to control or hurt them.

I made a tough decision right then and there. My son was not going to grow up in a house with two people who didn't respect each other, or even like each other.
As individuals, Raymond and I were decent enough, he simply had no idea how to be a good husband, and I was only *beginning* to learn how to be a good wife.

But together as parents, I knew that we would set a bad example for our son! I decided to go and live with Big Momma. I could help her and she could help me.

She refused to leave her home after Papa died. We were all trying to get her to go and live in one of those new old folks homes, *(senior building),* they were building across town. She would not go. This was the only home she'd known for most of her life, and she was not leaving it.
"William built this house for me and I am not leaving it until you all carry me out," she said when we presented the subject. This decision would solve a lot of problems.

She wouldn't be alone, and I could raise my son in a stress-free, hate free environment! My challenge now was Raymond. How would I convince him?

Did I actually think it would be as easy as all of that? Did I really think that Raymond was going to let me walk away with his son and not put up a fight? Well, I did, but I was crazy to think it would happen the way I wanted it to.

I prayed that he would see the logic in what I wanted to do. We had never been happy together. So why stay in a situation that neither one of us wanted.

As crazy as it sounded, I hoped that he would see this as an opportunity to be with his tramp that he was keeping across town! Now he could be with her openly and wouldn't need to sneak around anymore --telling himself that *"with my country and naive mind,"* I didn't know what was going on. He will soon learn that because I didn't say anything, did not mean that I didn't know what he was doing behind my back.

I will reason with him, that if he agreed to the separation, he would be free to do as he pleased, when he pleased. If he would not agree, we will let the court decide, and I plan to point out that adultery comes with a steep financial penalty.

I hoped he would agree and save us both a lot of time and trouble! When it was time for me to be released from the hospital with the baby, I reasoned with him that I should go home with Big Momma. She could help me with the baby while he was at work, because it was still hard for me to get around.

By now we were living in his parent's old mansion. We had a full time cook and housekeeper, and his mother was living with us because his father had passed away a year ago.

I was afraid that he would say that I had all the help I needed at home. But he said, "It will be okay if that is what you want." I was so shocked I almost lost my balance.

I just looked at him in disbelief, and then hurried into the wheelchair as fast as I could so that he would not have time to think about it and change his mind.

My sister Diane was there and my brother James, so if Raymond was planning to make a scene, I am sure he knew that after what just happened to Vanessa, it would be smart to let some more time pass.

Now all I had to do was to buy time until I could drum up the courage to actually **let him know** that I had left him.

Going to Big Momma's house was a good idea.
We all were still very raw from what had happened to Vanessa and Papa's passing. Having the baby there to take care of seemed to fill Big Momma with renewed energy.

She was moving around the house, taking care of the baby, feeding and bathing him. She was mostly taking care of him while I rested and tried to figure out my next steps in getting Raymond to agree to separate.

To my shock and surprise, Raymond was trying to be accommodating. He even hired a nurse to come in and help with the baby and housework during the day. My grandmother was energized, but she was 86, she could only do so much!

Finally the day came when my husband said that it was time for us to take our son home to live in his own house. I couldn't put it off any longer. I had to tell him the truth about how I was feeling about our marriage.

I tried to be sophisticated about the whole thing. I thought honesty was the only way to go right now.
I was counting on the fact that he was unhappily married also. It was my only hope that he would agree.

I was strategic in my timing; although my sisters knew of my plan, their husbands and my uncles did not. I asked them all to come to the house that day so we could have dinner.

I knew that if the house was full of my family, Raymond would not dare go off! How wrong could I have been? After we had all eaten and everyone started to make moves to leave, I signaled to my sisters to have their husbands to do little things like move suitcases and take out the trash.

I asked Raymond to come into Papa's study to talk with me for a moment. I went right into the fact that we were never happy. The marriage was not working for either of us, and we both knew it. The proof was Deborah Johns, his Mistress across town. We should stop making each other unhappy and separate. Our son should grow up in a house without fighting and yelling and unhealthy behavior.

His silence made me think that perhaps he was thinking about it, and that he was going to agree with me, until he turned to me with a twisted frown, and he called me "an ungrateful bitch!" Then, without another word, he hit me so hard that he knocked me over Papa's desk.

I hit the ground with a crash; lamp, pens, pencils and me, all crashing to the floor at the same time! Before I could catch my breath and get up, he was on me.

He picked me up by my collar and slapped me once, by the time he was raising his hand to hit me again, my uncles and sisters and their husbands were in the room and beating him like he stole something!

The scene was a horrible one, I believe the pain and frustration of what had happened to Vanessa was coming out of them, and because Roger took away their opportunity for retaliation, they were getting it on Raymond!

Was it stupid of him to hit me in my family home after we had just buried our loved one for the same thing? What was he thinking? Obviously he wasn't. It took Big Momma to break up the brawl. My brother-in-law and my brother put him in a chair and called Uncle William. I didn't want them to kill him, I just wanted a divorce!

I agree I didn't handle this situation entirely well. I should have been honest with him from the start, but where did I learn about honesty in relationships? All I knew about was survival! Big Momma dealt with my injuries while the men "dealt" with Raymond.

My sisters were trying to listen at the door to see if they could hear what was being said. There was nothing breaking, so we are sure that they were talking to him, and not killing him.

I don't know what the discussion was about, but I didn't see Raymond again until divorce court.

I never knew what the men in my family said to Raymond that day, but the court gave me full custody of Raymond Jr., with visitation granted to his father. As much as his posture showed that he did not agree, he didn't open his mouth to say a word. He just sat there looking like he was going to burst at any moment.

His mother was in court also. She did not bother to look at me. She just looked ahead, in that Queenly manner of hers and didn't show any emotions at all.

The last thing I remember was the judge say GRANTED! That was it, the deed was done. I was finished with this unhappy chapter in my life.

Good riddance! Although I was likely the most eligible match for Raymond in our town, as far as education and family background, his mother treated me as if I was not good enough for her son. I never developed a close relationship with her.

I was happy now that my interaction with her would be limited to short visits, and a once a year birthday party for Raymond Jr. Even with that limited contact, I was willing to allow two birthday parties, one for their family and one for mine, so we need not see each other until absolutely necessary!

One day when I was dropping the baby off for his visit, Raymond's mother did take the opportunity to tell me what a huge mistake I made in divorcing her son!

And how ignorant I was to break up my home and deny Raymond Jr., the opportunity to live in his own home, with his father, where he belonged.

At that moment something in me snapped -all of the pain, humiliation and frustration that this family had brought me for the past six years came pouring out of me. I told her "it would be over my dead body that I would ever allow my son to be a permanent part of her family circus!"

"She was the fool for putting up with her husband's cheating and disrespect for all of these years, and for what; money and a last name! How in the hell could she be so high and mighty, to judge me, while her husband and sons were making babies all over town, and not having enough class to try and keep their bad behavior a secret!"

I told her. "My son was going to grow up normal! In a loving house, where there was no shame and disrespect, no pain or humiliation and I will **never** have to answer questions for him like, why does daddy hurt mommy?"
"If you don't get **that**, then you are slower than I have always thought you were!" She stared at me with a blank look for a second, and then she said simply, "I knew my place."

"In my day for a woman to have **anything**, she had to go through a man." I said to her, "No, that was not the truth, and the fact that you believe it, is a sad commentary on your life! I feel sorry for you! "I walked away feeling renewed and freer than I had felt in years.

Raymond's mother was not a bad person, but like Big Momma, she was a victim of her times and circumstances. But unlike Big Momma, she didn't seem to realize that something was wrong, that things could be different.

I was more determined than ever to make it on my own as a single parent. Now I had to prove **to myself**, that my choice to divorce Raymond was the right one! (Like Big Momma used to say, no regrets!) I had to let go of my fears of being alone, and take a chance on the life I wanted to live.

One that was free of pain and humiliation, and the fear that I would end up like my Aunt Bee or Vanessa. I had to move pass the pain of my divorce. Although we never loved each other, Raymond was my first lover, and he was the father of my son, so I had emotions that were tied to him I was working through, and didn't understand.

I don't know what was worse, the pain of losing my marriage and a love in Raymond that I never actually had. Or facing the realization that my husband didn't love me enough to honor our marriage vows, that he didn't respect me; along with the shame of knowing that he cheated on me endlessly.

He fathered children all over town, with no regard to how it would affect me, or our marriage; like it didn't matter to him. Deep down I knew I had made the right choice. I had to learn to live through the pain and disappointment of what happened to us.

Now I know what people mean when they say "as if a weight has been lifted!" I was carrying more baggage than I ever realized. To finally have it behind me was a good feeling! *(Moving on)!* Although Raymond was paying alimony and child support, I wanted to find a job.

I didn't need the money, as much as I wanted something constructive to do. I have an MBA and had never actually used it. As it happens, Uncle Williams's wife was ready to retire from the family business.

I saw this as an opportunity to work and contribute to my family legacy, so we all decided I would train to take over her duties as business and operations manager.

What was it going to be like working with my mother each day? I noticed with all that has happened to our family, along with the passage of time, she has mellowed toward me.

She was not quite as distant "maybe it will not be so bad!" She surprised me by acting very much like a grandmother to my son. I supposed her issues were with me. I am happy that they did not flow over to R. J.

She would keep him for me sometimes without me asking her. She would pick him up, and take him to the park on Saturday afternoons with the other children. "Will wonders never cease?" Let's not get it twisted, I was nowhere close to having a real mother daughter relationship with her yet, but I think we developed an understanding!

I almost think that she respected my choice to leave Raymond, even if she did say that I was crazy to walk away from all of that wealth. She said, "Don't give up so easily, he will not live forever, you could have withstood it a few more years. After all, he didn't **actually** hit you until you made him angry!" I was in such a good place in my life right now even that nonsense didn't bother me; I just laughed it off, and to my surprise, so did she.

"A TIME TO LAUGH A TIME TO CRY"

I enjoyed working and making my own money. I was still living with Big Momma and a good thing because her health was starting to fail.

The child support and alimony that Raymond paid afforded us a nurse and housekeeper, so someone was with Big Momma and the baby all day while I worked.

My sister Diane would go over to the house most days to help out and take care of our mother. Finally, I had a life that was my own, making choices, taking care of my family, and not being afraid of what the day would bring.

As I was training in the family business, my cousin Neoshia, Uncle Anderson's daughter, was also. She was actually taking over the duties that my mother had as office manager. We were close in age and were very good friends, growing up and as women.

She moved back home from St. Louis with her two children after her divorce; same drama, cheating and beating. What was this; a sickness that men get along with the **X chromosomes?!** She was now my partner in crime. One good thing about living in a town with all of your family is there is never a shortage of babysitters.

We were still young women, and we wanted to have fun. We even went to St. Louis a couple of times to party with people "Nea" knew there. Different life, different me, I thought that I had learned a lot over the past six or seven years, and that I was ready for whatever was to come my way.
But life had a cruel way of tricking you about stuff like that. My lessons were just beginning!

Big Mamma was so ill now that a nurse had to be at the house around the clock, but Big Momma still didn't want to leave her home, and we respected her wishes.

There was nothing the doctors could do for her. She was older and I think she was tired. Her husband was gone, her parents, her best friends had also passed on. I think she was just ready to rest. After Sunday dinner, April 24, 1988, Big Momma was saying goodbye to her family.

She had each of the great-grandchildren brought to her. She hugged and kissed them, she seemed to say a prayer over each of them, and then gave the child back to his parents. She asked each of her children to come into the room, then her grandchildren, saying to us all, "I have gotten you as far as I can take you. I am tired now and I want to see my mother again."

After everyone left the room, I lingered a minute, because I wanted to ask her about **what if**. She smiled at me as if she knew my question before I asked it.

She said "Baby life is what you make of it each day. You have to live life and not worry about making mistakes. That is how you learn and grow in life."

"A mistake is a lesson waiting to be learned! Do not worry about your choices; just make the ones that feel right to you. Stop punishing yourself for things that are not your fault, like the circumstance of your birth."

"Wondering about **what if** is dreaming. You have to deal with **what is** and what is happening in front of you, right now, today-because now is all there is."

"Don't look back with regret. Forgive yourself and move forward. Worrying about what has happened, and what is going to happen is only going to make you scared and crazy.

There is simply nothing you can do about what is past, all you can do is try to make good choices for the future. Live baby, live and enjoy the blessing of the life God gave you."

"If I had it to do over again, I would not change one thing, because to change anything, could mean that I might not have anyone of you, I am tired now; I need to rest.

Turn out the light and turn my music show on for me, it helps me to sleep." As I turned out the light, and turned on the radio, I said "I love you Big Momma," she said, "I love you too baby, I love you too." Then my Big Momma went to sleep.

We buried Big Momma next to Papa, Aunt Bee, Vanessa and George, and too soon after her, my brother James. I will miss her so; I always felt that she was the only one who really cared about me, that I was never an embarrassment for her.

She loved me and I loved her, and now she was gone. What will I do without her? Who will I share my troubles with? But I must find the courage to do as she said.

There was my son to think about; I had to move on for him. Make sure that he was okay, and that he would not become his father's son! The question now was what to do with Big Momma and Papa's house. It was too big for the baby and me alone, and everyone else already had a house.

We didn't want to sell it. It was a part of our family history, our legacy, getting rid of it was out of the question. So what to do with it?

I decided to stay in the house as we tried to figure it out. There was no rush for me to move out. The house had no mortgage, and we were the only house for miles, so I had my privacy. We thought that Janet and her husband could move in with the three children because they had a small four-bedroom house. This could be more comfortable for them.

They would sell their house and use the money to expand the grocery store. In the meantime, I had to decide what I was going to do. I didn't want to move into Janet's house as suggested, Janet said that they could use the money from Papa's estate to expand the store, if I wanted the house.

Although her house was nice, and was small enough to work for Little RJ and me, I wanted a fresh start with my son, in our own place, surrounded by things I've chosen for myself, things that reflect who I was!

With my salary, alimony and child support, along with the money left to me by Papa, I had more than enough to buy one of those new town houses they were building across town.

Our company built the kitchen cabinets and painted the units; they were nice and spacious, with enough back yard for my son to play in. This was the change I needed to start my new life. This is the way I would go, fresh start, new life, new beginning!

Change can be good!

"SOMEDAY, CHANGE IS GONNA COME"

Diane, "Nea," her Brother A. J., my Uncle Anderson and Janet's husband, helped me to move into my new place. I was excited and scared at the same time.

I was trying to do what Big Momma said, live with my choices. This choice was one I was happy about. This was going to be a positive change for Raymond Jr. and me.

The townhouse has three bedrooms. My son had his room. I hired one of the artistic painters to make it a boys room, with his favorite characters painted on the wall.

My sister said I would regret it because, "when he grows up, he will change his alliances with cartoon characters! "No worries, I said to her, don't we OWN a decorating business? Get a grip; he is two and a half!"

My room was large and sunny, and I decided to make the third bedroom into a home office, with a sofa in it that could double as a daybed, just in case I had an overnight guest.

Although most of my furniture was new, many of the pieces that I was using for accenting my new digs are from Big Momma's house; lamps, side tables and other odds and ends.

I wanted a fresh start, but her things were antiques, *let's not be foolish!* The bedroom furniture she had was early nineteen century oak, expensive and built to last. I also took her dining room table and chairs: also old, but nice, classic.

Nea stayed over to help me to unpack. We were almost inseparable these days. Her daughter hung out with us, but her son Ryan wanted to be around his grandparents, and his little baby cousin.

Nea's brother, Anderson Jr. and his baby daughter, Madison were living with Uncle Anderson and Aunt Sue.

He was staying with them temporally until he could find a place, since he and his wife Tina were separated, and he had custody of his daughter. We were giggling and squealing like two schoolgirls. Nea's daughter was twelve years old and was old enough to take care of R.J., while we unpacked, and drank several glasses of wine, as we listened to the O'Jays on the CD player. She was as excited for me as I was for myself. She was more like a sister than a cousin.

Nea started to date again, but that was not me right now. Raymond and I had been divorced two years, but I needed more time to get to know **me**.

I was tired of men, I didn't want to have to decipher **man speak**; you know what I mean, new relationship language like *"if he meant what he said, when he said what he said, or did he mean something else and I didn't understand what he said"?!*

Not at all tempted! It was exhausting! I just didn't have the energy to deal with it. I was tired of being disappointed by men, and I did not want to be in a position where I could get hurt, so I stayed to myself. Raymond Sr., remarried not a year after our divorce was final. I wasn't that suspired by the marriage, but I was surprised by who he married.

I thought for sure he would marry the woman he was cheating on me with for years, Deborah.

I suspected that her youngest was his child, but he continued to deny it. His new wife was a local girl. I remember her from high school. Her name was Shelia Williams. I think her father was the minister of a church or something.

Not at all someone I would imagine Raymond with. I would not think that she was his type, you know what I mean; *she was respectable*.

Around school she was always quiet, a bookworm type. She didn't go to many parties, and she was very plain looking back in school, and plain looking now. *His mother will have a great time pulling her together!*

I didn't even know they knew each other. Since I was never really in love with my husband, I honestly didn't care who he ended up with!

When they would come to my house to pick up RJ, Sheila was polite and acted almost scared, like she was afraid to say or do anything that would bring attention to her.

I guess my brother George was right when he would tell me to "respect yourself. Be a lady at all times, because there are the girls that the boys would play around with and the girls they would bring home to meet their momma and marry!"

In spite of our very messy divorce, Raymond and I managed to develop a quite truce.

We didn't fight or argue anymore, *(what would we have to fight about)*, but he still acted as if he hated me. That was his problem; I had moved on, thank God. He was Shelia's problem now, not mine. Good luck, she was going to need it!

Neoshia and I were planning to take the children to dinner and put them to bed early one Friday night after work, and then have a stiff drink at my house. But she cancelled when her "gentleman friend," called and asked if they could get together. I was okay with it. I was tired.

It had been a long week. Going to my place and putting my feet up worked just fine for me. She had gone out with this guy a couple of times. He seemed nice. A little short for my taste, and a bit too hood, *but to each his own.*

She said they were going to a new nightclub outside of town. The club was owned by the same family that owned a popular nightclub closer to home in **The Bottoms**.

They were going for a drink and check out the latest nightspot around. For years we went to The Bottoms to party. It was close and it was a place where the young people in our town would go to have a wild time.

It is where my mother and her siblings used to go and party, back in their day. My mother recalled that it was where she went out with her sister, Bertha for the last time before she was murdered.

She said it was years before she could step a foot in the place and not break down and cry. *I am sure that since it was also the same club she went to with my father the night she met him, didn't help her emotions either!*

The grandson of the original owner was running the place now. It has changed a bit since the old days, but still specialized in great music and cheap liquor. Now he opened up a new club 30 or 40 miles out-side of town.

He was trying to draw people from Jackson and New Orleans who didn't want to make the trip all the way to Madisonville each weekend; though many did because the place was so well known.

He saw this as an opportunity for growth, and wanted to cater to a more exclusive crowd. Of course I know all of this because the young owner and I went to high school together. We dated for about five seconds during the summer before I was married, when Raymond found out about his first son. He still lived in town and we were still friendly.

I could have married **him**, but I was not one for the nightlife; and I thought I was in love with Raymond, I believe he and I were predestined!

Nea suggested that I should come with them because he had a cute friend who wanted to meet me.

I was not the least bit interested. I was still in my own zone. Didn't want a man right now, I didn't feel like the drama, *don't men always bring drama?*

I told her no thanks, but she should come over in the morning to have breakfast with me and tell me about her hot date! She laughed and said she would.

I offered to keep the kids, but she said they were with her parents for the weekend. I said goodbye to my cousin and friend. Kissed her and promised to make French toast for breakfast! It didn't bother me one bit that Nea wanted to be with her new guy instead of me on a Friday night. I was becoming quite comfortable with my own company these days.

Raymond was celebrating his birthday this weekend and wanted R.J., to be there with him, so I was home alone for the evening. I made a hot bath, poured myself a tall drink and went to sleep early.

The next morning when Nea didn't call me, I was mad as hell. I took the time and made all that damn French toast, bacon and sausage with fruit on the side, just the way she likes it. I wanted to keep her talking so I could hear all about this date she dumped me to go on!

Frustrated and not wanting to waste the food, I called Diane to come over to help me eat all of the breakfast I prepared for Nea and could not possibly eat alone.

She brought Janet with her; we ate, and had coffee. We sat and talked for a while. It felt good. We had not been together as just girls in a long time. We needed the impromptu visit! Now it was three o'clock and still no word from Nea.

I called Uncle Anderson and his wife Sue answered the phone. She said that they had been trying to reach Nea also, and were wondering if she was with us.

I told her that I had not spoken with her since last night. She had promised to have breakfast with me, but she was a no-show. This was not at all like her. She was a responsible daughter and parent.

Unlike my sister Phyllis, she would never drop her children off on her family and not check on them, she would not worry her parents by not checking-in. Something was wrong there had to be a reason for her behaving so out of character.

We had Uncle William call the police station. Now he was retired, but still had connections and influence at the precinct. The Madisonville police department put out a missing persons call on Nea after going to her house and finding her car there, but no sign of her.

They contacted the highway patrol, and Uncle William asked detectives that he knew to go by the nightclub she went to the evening before. I was thinking how lucky it was that she told me where she was going; maybe she was in an accident. At least we could tell them where to look first.

Uncle William said they would check with the Highway Patrol and find out if there had been any car accidents near the club, and they would check the hospitals.
We all gathered at Big Momma's house where Janet was living now with her family and waited to hear.

When the detectives called Uncle William and said the body of a young woman had been found in a ditch between Madisonville and Jackson, he didn't say anything to Uncle Anderson or Aunt Sue about this new information. He didn't want to worry them in case it was not her.

He didn't want her distressed parents to worry any more than they already were. He told us to keep quiet until he returned, and could find out more about what was going on. The detectives knew before my uncle reached the crime scene that the dead girl was Nea!

Papa was gone, and Uncle William was retired, but our family legacy was still strong in this town. Although Madisonville had grown over the years, at the heart it was still a small town, and my family helped to make it what it had grown to be today. The detectives said that Nea had not been **badly** beaten, but the police report said that there were bruises on her forearms and around her neck.

There were no signs of a struggle at the crime scene, so they suspected that she was killed someplace else, and driven there. She had been shot, once in the head, and dumped on the side of the road, like trash!

The hunt was on for the man she had gone on the date with. I had only met him a couple of times, but I was able to give the police a description of him.

Ronald Walker moved to Madisonville from Los Angeles. He was a barber in a local barbershop. He didn't have family here in Madisonville. He told Nea that he was just passing through, liked what he saw, and decided to stay. **(Is that not a big red flag)?**

He had only been in town a few months before he met Nea at a party with friends. I was with her that night as well. I have not observed them together as a couple, because it had only been a couple of months since they started dating. I have no idea what type of relationship they had, or how they interacted together.

But Nea was not stupid, so he must have been acting okay with her. So what was this? They weren't in love; they didn't have a real relationship, what was this about?

There couldn't have been enough passion between them in the two months that they had known each other, and the couple of dates they had gone on to cause this kind of violence.

I thought I was beginning to have the answers about life, love, and relationships, but this; this was too much. How could anyone understand this?

Once again, my family was dealing with the death of someone we loved that was lost at the hands of a man. Killing her with no more regard for her life than he would have for a stray dog! Janet said "we are not sure that it was him.

 Maybe they had both been victims of a robbery or something, after all, why would he do this to her? He hardly knew her? There had to be another explanation!

This could not be relationship violence, because there was not a relationship!" With the resources of all of the police forces between Madisonville and Jackson-- Ronald was apprehended rather quickly.

Nea was the niece of a local policeman. She was one of their own. They were not going to stop until they caught him. "He didn't have a chance," said Janet's husband! *It seems neither did Nea!*
Janet's husband and Nea's brother A.J., went to the police station with Uncle Anderson, while Uncle Will stayed with the detectives at the crime scene, trying to determined what happen. We all stayed with Aunt Sue and tried to console her. *God, not again; why didn't I go with her? Could I have prevented this from happening?*

Of course, no one was going to sleep. We all stayed at Janet's house with the children. We sat up to wait for the men. We had to give Aunt Sue a sedative to calm her down. It was barely three years since Vanessa's murder, now this!

When Janet's husband came home, he had the full story. He looked like he had been in a fight --*but we will get to that later.* Damon, Janet's husband began to tell us what happened to Nea as Ronald had confessed it, and what was told to the police by witnesses.

He said "Nea and Ronald made it to the club as originally planned, but when they got there, it was not as nice as they thought it was going to be.

Although it was a new spot, and very different from the club in The Bottoms, the crowd was pretty young and Nea wanted to leave." It was a 45-minute drive to get there, so her date suggested that they stay and have at least one drink since they had come all this way, and then drive back to Madisonville. Well, instead of one drink, Ronald had a few.

Nea knew he was in no condition to drive because she asked the waiter to cut him off. She knew that he could never make it home this way. It was too far and he was too drunk. She asked for the waiter's assistance to get Ronald's car keys so that he would not try to drive, and kill them both! *What irony.*

Because he was so drunk, and it was so late, and he couldn't drive, he suggested they stay in town at a motel near the club. Nea ran into a couple of people she knew at the club that night, just before she was trying to leave. They saw what was happening and offered to drive her home.

She told them no. She didn't want to leave her friend in that condition alone. She would drive them home as soon as she got a hold of his car keys, which he refused to surrender. They asked her if she was sure, she said yes, she would be fine. They would be leaving shortly also.

Ronald was determined to get Nea to that motel. He told her that if she didn't want to walk home, she would go with him. She yelled at him "to hell with you! I am going to ask the bartender to call me a cab, I am done with you!"

He started to laugh. He said to her, "Okay, get in the car girl, I was just playing with you." If she got in the car, he would give the keys to her and allow her to drive them home.

But when they got in the car, witnesses said that Ronald was behind the wheel, not Nea. That Nea and the guy appeared to be arguing. The witness said that from what he could see, Nea tried to get out of the car, but he drove off before she could get the door open.

That was all he could see before they were gone. Under pressure, Ronald related that Nea was upset and wanted him to let her drive. He said that he thought they should stay over and drive back in the morning.

He said she began to yell at him, "Who in the hell did he think he was? She was not going to a motel with him, and he either needed to take her home, or take her to the bus station and she would get herself home!

She was not going to go to a hotel with him for a couple of cheap drinks, and a bucket of chicken! Who did **he** have **her** confused with?!" He said this made him angry. He was sure it was the alcohol, because he was very angry with her for saying that. He said that he just wanted to shut her up!

He didn't understand why she was making such a big deal about spending the night out. She said that her parents had her kids, and she wasn't a young girl.

She had been married and divorced so she was not innocent! *I am guessing it was at this point that Janet's husband got into a fight with this fool!*

As I said before, my uncle and family still had pull in this town, although they had to keep Uncle Anderson and A.J., away from Ronald, Damon was allowed in the room when the police were talking to him.

Against the law, yes, but who was going to tell?
When they pulled Damon off of Ronald, he continued with his story. Angry now so Ronald didn't hold anything back.

He said that he told her to quit acting up and just go with him; after all, he had spent good money on her on all those dates that she needed to do something for him!

(The fact that he had said this ignorant mess out loud makes me want to go and have a fight with him myself, so I guess it was her fault that he killed her)!

He said she slapped him, and he slapped her back. The bruises on her arms were a result of him trying to hold her back. He told her that he had heard about the King family. That they thought they were all that, but from where he sat she was just another "horny" divorced woman trying to get a nut!

Nea hit at him again, and began to yell at him. This time he grabbed her around her neck and began to choke her to shut her up. When she broke free of him, she managed to get out of the car. She said, "I am going to call the police! When my uncle gets a hold of you, you are going to pay for this!"

What Nea didn't know about this man she was with is that he had left California fleeing the law. This was not his first violent incident, or likely his second, he had another assault charge under his belt.

He said he didn't want to go back to jail. When he could not get her to stop screaming for the police, he grabbed at her but missed. Before he knew it, he took his gun out and shot her.

He dumped her body a few miles up the road. He was going to bury her he said, "but I didn't have a shovel!" So he just left her there and drove away!

Since he had a record and was wanted by the law, now in two states, it wasn't hard for the police to track the car he was driving, because it wasn't his- it was *borrowed* from a friend in California, and was reported stolen several months before.

The highway patrol arrested him trying to cross over the state line into Louisiana.

That was it? My cousin was dead and gone and for what; because this fool was running from the law? I was so angry I could not see straight!

Now **I know** that I was done with men. All men are fools. They are so dangerous they should not be walking around without a sign around their neck; like a warning label so that women will know what they are getting into.

How can a woman, any woman protect herself from this? How do you know what you are getting when you go on a date, or have a conversation with someone you meet?
This was madness! I was beginning to see not only are the women in my family cursed, all women are cursed, and MEN ARE THE CURSE!

This is one thing that Big Momma didn't tell me. **Big Momma never said that this could happen.** A random man could take your life, simply because he had an ego. Kill you, with no thought to what it would mean to the people you are leaving behind; your parents, your children, your friends and your siblings!

Those men don't seem to accept that we women do matter. That we have a right to say NO! God, why does this happen to women? What is wrong with this world?!

Why is it that men only view woman as objects, not as real people? Something they can use, and then throw away when they were done?

Where did this behavior come from, is there a special school that men go to that women don't know about, where they learn how to mistreat and disrespect women?

A secret place where they get lessons on treating us like crap-- like we don't matter, that our lives don't matter? And then teach them how to feel justified in their bad behavior, because somehow we women did not get with the program they laid out, and what happens to us as a result of not following the program, we deserve, that it is our own fault!

"NOWHERE TO RUN – NOWHERE TO HIDE"

The murder of my cousin, along with Ronald's trial, knocked the wind out of me. It took almost a year after his arrest to bring him to trial. I was broken hearted and dazed. My world was spiraling out of control.

I had to get away from Madisonville so I could catch my breath. My emotions were borderline hysterical. Since Uncle Anderson had retired and was devastated over the murder of his daughter. I could not ask him to come back to work and help me, and now A.J., was gone to. I was the only member of the family left working in the business. I was basically running the company alone.

Luck for me, Papa had the foresight to hire Billy and his family all those years ago, to help with the business, because I could never manage all this on my own!

As much as I wanted to get out of town, I was not sure if I could get away; now that the responsibility of my family's livelihood rested on my shoulders.

Although he had retired also, Billy and his wife promised to keep things in order for me while I went away. They recognized my need for escape. I knew they were capable of managing Kings Decorating without me, so I jumped at the chance to get out of town.

I did not plan to be away very long, just long enough to regain my sanity and a glimmer of hope, so that I could live through this new tragedy.

I wanted to try and believe in what Big Momma would say in times of trouble, "God will not give you more than you can bear," but I was feeling as if I had reached my limit.

I decided to take a trip to Georgia to visit with my college roommate Jennifer (Jenny) Rawlings and her family.

Jennifer was a white girl who knew more about the civil rights movement than most black people. She was my friend in school, in spite of our different backgrounds.

≈

I know in many of the other chapters I talked about separation of the races, but it was testimony to the times in our lives that dictated race relations. The fact is that my family was not racist, remember my great- grandfather was white, and my grandmother was so light she could have passed for white if she chose to. So no, we were not racist; we were simply living in the time we were born in.

≈

After the highly publicized disappearance of those three Civil Rights workers, who went missing and were later found murdered in Philadelphia, Mississippi, (just 45 miles from Madisonville) in 1964, she thought the world was in need of change. So she was determined to be a part of the solution.

Her family, like mine wanted to throw money at the problem, so their daughter would not embark on this suicidal crusade! Her family was supporters of the civil rights movement, and donated money in Atlanta to the local up and coming NAACP. From the look of her Grandfather when I first met him, I thought he was surly the Imperial Wizard of the local KKK! Although he was very old, he looked menacing; but as it turned out, he was a strong supporter of the movement to desegregate schools in Georgia.

He was a member of the ***Sibley Commissions***, which laid the foundation for the end of the resistance to desegregation in the State of Georgia. Although many of the members supported segregation, he pushed for change, *looks can be deceiving!*

Still, her family did not want Jenny to be mixed up in the violent demand for change that the civil rights movement brought with it in our country. But there was no reeling her in.

Without her parents knowing it, she changed her college roommate assignment. Jenny forged her mother's signature and requested an African American roommate.

She was determined to be a part of the change against racism. Like her grandfather, Jenny didn't just talk the talk –she walked the walk. If there was a sit-in, stand-in or lay-in, Jenny was either at the front of the line, or one of the organizers.

I often thought the girl had a death wish. She spent more time in jail than in class. Unlike my roommate, I did not have the luxury of being a rebel, or an activist. Her dedication and commitment to the cause shamed me. It was the way that she was so involved in the fight for equal rights for my people.

But I had to stay focused, because of my fragile relationship with my mother and my situation, (engaged to marry into a founding family in our town), I didn't have the liberty of being in a position to shake things up!

I was determined to finish school, and of course I could not step outside of my lane, and do anything that would make my mother's statements true about me *being no good like my father*. I could not take the chances that Jenny did. I tried to help out where I could. I would help her paint signs and print flyers, even pass out a few, but no marching and no hell raising.

Jennifer and her boyfriend Thomas were planning to go to law school after college. They wanted to be civil rights lawyers. In college, they had that in common. They were both committed to change the world.

If it were the early 60s, she would have been a hippy. She preferred to be compared to Angela Davis, instead of to Patty Hurst, because she was following her own mind, not being brainwashed!

After graduation, we kept in touch, but never as much as we promised we would on the day we said goodbye. Jenny was in my wedding, and I was in hers. I was also the godmother of her oldest daughter, Jennie.

We would send cards and letters during the appropriate times; Christmas, birthdays, death and birth announcements, and the occasional phone call.

After Vanessa's death and Big Momma's, Jenny encouraged me to come and stay with her and Tom for a while. They married after law school, and now lived in her family's estate, located in a small town called Fairfield Georgia, population roughly 68,000 residents.

Like us, her family was one of the original settlers in the town. Her Father passed away the same year as Papa; her mother still lives with her and Thomas.

She and Tom both practiced family law in the town where they live, and where her grandfather was once the Mayor. Jennifer is now Deputy Mayor.

She called her home, a farm, but it was *an estate*! The place is so large that her mother has her own wing. When I visit her, R.J., and I will be in a guest house two miles from the main house. We will take a golf cart to the main house when we wanted to be there.

When we were in school Jenny's parents thought that she was being eccentric when she would drag her black roommate home for holidays. And someday she would outgrow her *fascination with Black people*! But she was sincere about her passion, and we remained friends.

After the different tragedies in my life, when she would invite me to visit, I refused. There was too much happening with my family to leave town.

However, this time, after Nea's murder, I had to get out. I had to be away from the place that brought me so much fear and pain, if only for a few days or weeks.

Jenny gave me an open invitation; I could stay as long as I needed to! After the trial ended, I called Jennifer to let her know that I was going to come and visit, and that I would bring Little R.J., with me. She was thrilled because she had not seen him since his baptism, (she was his godmother).
The distance between our town and Jenny's was about 300 miles. Less than an hour by plane, but I decided to drive.

Not only did I want to have the time alone to clear my head, but since I was taking little R.J., I thought it would be easier than flying alone with the baby. Along with all of the extra things I would need to take with me to keep him comfortable. The baby seat and the stroller, the baby bag, luggage; *damn, single parenting was a bitch!*

I still had my little red mustang convertible, although I didn't drive it every day. I held on to it because I have a passion for antiques, now it was a valuable classic.

Most days, to get around town I drove a company car, a red Toyota pickup truck, *don't hate*! It was a small truck, just two seats, and it was cute as a button, and yes, I love red! After I married Raymond, he bought me a Cadillac sedan for my wedding present.

His family had a contract with the local dealer; Cadillac was the official car for *"R.R. Willis and Sons Mortuary."* Of course, that was the car of choice for his family. His family members all drove a Cadillac.

But that was never my favorite style of car. It reminded me too much of a pimp car, or a car suited for an old man, someone like Raymond's father. But my pleas fell upon deft ears, for years, I was forced to conform.

After a time, I guess he grew weary of me looking lost in that huge car, he did concede and bought a BMW for my birthday, then another for our fifth and final wedding anniversary gift. When I knew I was pregnant, Raymond purchased a Volvo station wagon so that I could travel comfortably with the baby. I won that car in the divorce- **I drove the Volvo to Georgia.**

When I arrived at Jenny and Tom's house, he was not at home. He was in Atlanta working on a case. It was just us and the children. She and Tom hand four children, three girls and one boy. Her children were *earthy* like their mother, smart, secure and uninhibited.

She raised them to know their own mind, and to speak it. Little R.J., would laugh at the way they would debate with her and *rationalize* with their mother, on the practicality of them not bathing daily, or not eating certain vegetables. He would look at me for a reaction and my return look was, **"Don't you even think about it"!**

They had a nanny that lived on the property. She would take R.J., with her when the children went to the park or to play outside. Since the three older children were in school, R.J. and little Thomas spent the day with the nanny; this gave me plenty of time to myself. I needed this time to begin to heal. The privacy of the guest house was perfect.

After all that has happened in such a short time, I was not feeling very optimistic about life and the future. I was honestly wondering if I would make it through this new tragedy. I was still mourning Vanessa and Big Momma, now Nea, my heart felt as if it were going to explode!

Being at Jenny's house was comfortable for me. The guest house had all of the luxuries of home, and more.

I could have the cook send my meals down from the main house if I didn't want to come up for dinner; which I did most nights after Tom returned from Atlanta, so that he and his family could have time alone.

When Tom was away, Jenny and I talked for hours on end; sometimes going to bed just before dawn. We had so much to catch up on. We talked about what was happening in our lives over the years since school. My divorce, her father and grandfather's passing, and the deaths of Vanessa and Nea.

One evening after dinner, when the children were in bed and we were sitting outside in front of her outdoor fireplace, enjoying an *excellent* bottle of wine, Jennifer confessed to me that Tom was verbally abusive!

He had a very bad temper and would yell and scream, *often*-not only at her but also at the children! By now, she said, that he has graduated to throwing and breaking things to make his point! I was shocked! I could not believe what I was hearing from Jenny. Telling her about my family gave her the courage to speak out. She said no one knew, but her mother and his sister. She was ashamed to tell anyone else.

Like the women in my family, they encouraged **her** to **change her** behavior to make the marriage work!
In school, Tom was always quiet, and Jenny so outgoing. He followed Jenny around like a blind love sick puppy. I guess you don't know someone until you have seen him at his worst!

I always thought this type of behavior only happened in black families. "White people were far too proper to yell and curse at women and children," especially their own family member. So this thing did not have boundaries. Anyone and everyone could be affected; every race, everyplace, anyone, can be the victims of domestic violence.

Because of what my family and I lived through, I had no tolerance for a man who mistreated his wife and children.
I was afraid for Jenny and I told her so. She insisted that Tom would never go as far as the men in my stories.

I asked her why she felt that way, "because Tom was white? So was Bradley," I reminded her!

She prickled at the comparison, and said, "You know better than that, I know my husband. He is a good man. It's just that he has been under a lot of pressure lately, first with the election and now with this big case in Atlanta."
Sounding defensive and protective, she said, "The stress causes him to act out of character sometimes.

With the election done, and now that I am settled in office; a bit of his stress is eliminated. When this tough case is over, his bad behavior will pass! I know it will, he will be his old self again." *(Still defensive)!*

I told her that I hoped and I prayed that she was right. I lost far too much to this crime and I did not want to lose her!
I said "you and Tom are educated people. Perhaps you could get some professional help.

Talk with someone, like a therapist about the problems you are having, before things get any worse!" From what I have experienced, it always gets worse.
(This is 1990 and there are still no laws to govern relationship violence in the United States. The violence against woman act was not written into law until 1994. In 1990 there was no family violence specific counseling).

She insisted that this was not abuse since it was not physical violence, he was not hitting her.

"He would never hurt me or the children! He was only yelling and screaming and throwing a few useless trinkets! Surely you don't consider him abusive!"

I reminded her that Raymond hit me one time after all of the years we were married, and once was one time too many! "Life was going to always bring pressures, how someone responds under pressure is a true testament to their character! Yelling and screaming at little children because of work pressure was inexcusable behavior!"

All of this certainly confirmed that I never really knew Tom. If he was capable of this bad behavior, what else might he do? I think deep down Jennifer knew I was right. No amount of pressure should make someone behave so out of character. Obviously, this is who Tom was, but I did not push.

I made her promise to get help, and to please keep me posted about what was happening with her. I also made her promise me that the first time he hit her or one of the children she was out of there! "Get help Jenny; please, before it's too late!"

I left Jenny's house after staying there for three weeks. Part of my decision to leave was because I couldn't be around Thomas without wanting to ***throw a few trinkets*** at his ass, and part because it was time to go home.

I could not run from my problems, I had to go home. I went back to Madisonville to face my own demons. But I was surer now, than ever that I was done with relationships.

There was not a doubt in my mind, that I would never be happy with a man! Big Momma was right; the women in our family would never have a happy relationship with a man, and it seemed that neither would many of the other women in my life! What a sad legacy!

"LIVE LAUGH LOVE"

If it were not for my son, I am positive that I would not have survived the past few years. Too much pain, too much loss, life should not be this difficult!

But I had to move on; I had to live for R.J., he needed me and I could not let him down. Now, my family was counting on me to hold it all together, not just for our family, but the business as well.

How did I manage to find myself at the head of the King family business? If anyone said this to me ten years ago, I would have laughed in their face. Said they were out of their minds, remembering I was the wild one!

The one that was out of control, *now* I am the one everybody is looking to for strength and direction. Life is nothing if not unpredictable!

One month after the trial was over for Nea's murder, I went back to work at the family business, and things were beginning to get back to a normal routine. Work, home, motherhood (not in that order)!

Ronald received life in prison for the murder of my cousin Neoshia, without the possibility of parole.
I promised that I would be at every parole hearing and write a letter to the court, the parole board, the governor, anyone, and everyone who might influence his release!

I promised Nea, every year on the anniversary of her murder to make sure there were no slip ups, and they let the fool out for good behavior or something like that.

No way, no how was he ever getting out of prison as long as I was alive! Her children went back to St. Louis to live with their father; my uncle and aunt were broken hearted about that also. This was a very bad time for the King Family.

But we pushed on in spite of all of the losses that we suffered over the past few years.

Billy's daughter came into the business to take over the job that Nea was doing. She was a nice girl, but a little overweight if you ask me, *(what? I said I was growing, I am still a work in progress)*. I will admit that she was hard working and well organized!

She was married to one of our painters. Aunt Jamie called them "decorators," but they were painters!

She was very talkative, I was happy that I had a door to my office. It was not that I didn't enjoy talking with her about her husband, her children, what she was going to cook for dinner, why the baby was sick; **enough already!** *(Sorry I am still a bit fragile)!* If I appear a little bitter, I am, sorry, there was so much change going on I could barely keep up.

I was still struggling to maintain control of my life and my senses after all that we had been through! Just being sane was a struggle. But I will get it together; **I am Peaches King after all!** Along with their daughter, Billy and Ella's oldest son was also working for the company now.

I am sure that Billy was protecting the investment of his time and talents by incorporating his children into the business. Sadly, right now I was the only King working in the company that my grandfather built. Uncle Anderson retired and his son Anderson Jr., Nea's brother moved to Atlanta. He said that he wanted no part of this town! Although he kept in touch with his parents, he wanted nothing to do with Madisonville Mississippi! He also had unhappy relationship memories of Madisonville. Not only was he living with the pain of his sister's murder, but his wife was nuts!

Unlike my sister Phyllis, she did not need alcohol as an excuse to act a fool, she was born crazy.

She worked in the company, but took a leave of absence after she had a baby, and her crazy behind didn't come back to work, *ever!* She said she "was too weak to work; **childbirth had caused her to be disabled!"**

Like with most of us, A.J., met his wife in high school. Although she was *from the wrong side of the tracks,* she was smart and ambitious. She won a scholarship to Hampton University in Virginia. Her major was business in marketing, she had an MBA. She was determined to leave her past behind her and surpass the rural area she grew up in.

She was a very pretty girl. She looked more Spanish than black. I would hear the men say that **she had a body by Fisher,** whatever that meant. But A.J. fell in love with her because she was so smart. He said "she wanted to go places," and he admired that about her. They kept in touch all through college; he would go and visit her as often as he could. But something happened to her when she was away at school.

Her behavior took a drastic change. She went from quite to crazy! She would come with A.J. to our family gathering for special holidays, like Christmas and Thanksgiving.

We notice during those visits that she stayed with Aunt Sue without going to be with her own family. Although she was quite in high school, she was friendly, but now when she was around, she would sit looking distracted, not saying much.

When we tried to engage her in conversation she gave quick answers, and looked angry because we were trying to talk to her. As if she resented having to be here.

After she received her master's degree, she worked in Virginia for a short time at a marketing firm. The next thing we knew A.J. was going to get her from Virginia, announcing that they were getting married. Two years later their daughter was born.

Uncle Anderson brought her into the business; I am sure with prompting from his son. She had my poor cousin by the noise. He was so much in love with this woman he couldn't think straight. Being married to Tina was a second job for him.

He was constantly trying to appease her, just to keep her calm. *If this is what she was like in front of us, I was afraid to imagine what she might be like behind closed doors!*

He was either apologizing to us about her bad behavior, or making excuses for her absence at family functions.

He didn't need to apologize to me; I did not miss her crazy ass she was not around, because she always brought drama with her! *(By now everyone knows how much I hate drama)!*

Someone in the family seemed to be doing or saying something to offend her every time we saw her, and she was not shy about making a scene. She would go straight loud and belligerent for no reason.

Because most of the time no one else would witness these assaults, we never knew how to act around her. Speaking to her could set her off. She would start screaming and yelling that someone said or had done something that offended her in some way. It could be male or female. Any one of my siblings, my aunts, the children; no one was immune from assaulting Tina!

We tolerated her outrageous behavior because she was A.J.'s wife, but we could only look past so much foolishness before it became too much!

True to form of the women in the King family, on more than one occasion he had to get her out of the room *fast*, before one of us grabbed her by all of that hair, and dragged her out of the house with it! For no reason **we** could identify, she would begin yelling at the children, one of our husbands, or anyone near her, just out of the blue!

Screaming that they touched her or made a threatening gesture toward her; (Crazy heifer)! *What is it with this family and relationships?* Big Momma would say, *"Y'all sure do know how to pick 'em!"* Knowing what I know now about human nature, I believe she was suffering from some type of chemical imbalance, because there was no basis for her behavior.

She was right about having a baby disabling her. She really did go off the deep end after she had their daughter Madison. Whatever was causing her to behave this way got worse after their daughter was born.

I believe that it was *bipolar disorder* or *postpartum-depression, on steroids!* A.J., said that he would come home from work, and she would be on the phone talking to her friends or listening to music and singing loud, while the baby would be in her crib crying. Tina would act as if she could not hear her!

If it were not for our family influence, she would have gone to jail a long time ago. Aunt Sue, (A.J.'s, mother), who was more ladylike and sophisticated than any woman I ever met, (besides Aunt Jamie), used to say that A. J. needed to "take her ass to the Nuthouse and drop her off!"

The last straw for A. J. was when she put the baby in the bathtub, and walked away. When A. J., got home from work that day and asked her where the baby was, because he did not see her, even when he checked her crib; he became concerned, but got no answer from his wife.

Then walking past the bathroom, he saw her in the tub. Her Mother's deranged behind told him she forgot she was there. While her baby was in the tub unattended, she told him, "She was *just* on the porch smoking a cigarette!"

"What was he so upset about, it's not like I left her home alone!" *(Which she had done before)!* When A.J. found his little daughter sitting in the adult tube of water, he freaked- luckily, he got there in time to save her.

When he was trying to get the baby out of the tube, Tina charged at him, like she did not understand that he was saving the baby or something!

During the tussle, the baby fell back in the tub and almost drowned, he had this fool on his back while he was trying to retrieve her from the water!

There was never any explanation from her as to why she jumped on him that day. We never understood her motives for attacking him when he was not only saving their baby, but her as well. My mother thought she was trying to get him to hit her so that she could divorce him, and get a big alimony and child support payday. *Leave it to my mother to come up with a conspiracy!* I for one did not think Tina was that smart.

Book smart, yes, no common sense, that type of plan required thinking. I don't believe she had it in her.

If that *was* the case, she obviously did not think that plan through. I believe she was jealous of A.J.'s love for his daughter. Unlike most women who would appreciate a man's love for his child, she resented it.

She could have killed her own baby playing crazy; and for what? Money and a divorce settlement, even she was not that out of touch!

She must have forgotten who his family was. Again, if that *was* her plan, we had enough lawyers on retainer that she never would have gotten a dime anyway.

Besides, A.J. was not the only witnesses to her erratic behavior. We all had seen her throw a fit more than once. So did other employees at King's Decorating, she would never have succeeded in getting money from us.

Who was the Judge going to believe, all of us or her? For child endangerment, alone A.J. had her ass. But he did not want to press charges.

He told the police and the hospital that Tina left the bathroom just long enough to get a clean bath towel, and the baby fell back into the tub! Because he called 911, the police and the hospital had to file a report. Because of her affiliation with our family, Tina did not go to jail; she went to a mental hospital. I suspect she should have been taken to rehab!

Poor A.J. did not want his child's mother to go to prison, but he knew that she had problems, and something needed to be done about her, before the child was seriously hurt or worse. Since his family kept her out of jail, A.J. made her sign away her parental rights, and made her promise to never try to be a part of their life, until Madison was old enough to decide for herself, if she wanted her mother in her life or not.

Hopefully by that time, she would have gotten the help she needed. Some might think this was harsh, but in my mind, he was very generous, she could have killed her baby!

He gave her too many chances over the years to get it together; her behavior was putting him and their baby in danger; she had to go!

As crazy as Tina acted, I know all of this broke his heart. Unlike his father, A.J. grew up in a home where his parents loved each other. His family had a healthy and loving relationship. He was never influenced by family violence, other than the stories about Big Momma and Papa that we all grew up hearing about.

He did not participate in violence against women. He wanted the same life for his wife and his family, the same loving environment that he grew up with.

Sadly, even the men were not immune from being victims of relationship madness, *the curse continues! (In reverse)!*

A few months after that happened, his sister was murdered. A.J. told his father "if I stay in this town another day he would kill someone," he could not take it anymore. He took his baby daughter and moved away.

Like I said, this was a very bad year for the King family! In less than a year, Uncle Anderson and Aunt Sue lost their son, daughter and all three of their grandchildren.

So, in walked Ralph James to take his place at work. It was all about the business right now! That might sound harsh, but remember; King's Decorating had at least seventy employees. There were many families besides our own, who relied on us keeping it together, in spite of our personal tragedies. Ralph was Billy's son; he came to work in the company to not only replace A.J., but Uncle Anderson as well, (Yes, the man was that good)!

He was a quiet man, like his father. He was divorced and moved back to Madisonville three years ago. (Seemed that the 80's were not a good time for marriage and relationships for anyone)! He went to High school with Raymond and me at Madison High. He was in the class ahead of me with Raymond. He was also on the basketball team like Raymond. That is where the similarities ended.

He was a nice guy, a little bit country like his dad; polite and always smiling, always a gentleman. He went to college in Louisiana; stayed and married a girl there, but he moved back home to help his father in **our business** after his divorce.

He was in business with his wife's father in New Orleans. I guess after the divorce that arrangement no longer worked for them. He did not have any children with his wife that I knew of.

I do not know what happened between him and his wife. He did not talk about it, and I didn't ask him. He was always private, even in high school; he kept his business to himself, and was protective of his girlfriends. The other boys in the school thought it made him a "chump" to be thoughtful and respectful, but all of the girls thought it was sweet.

As much as they would say to us that he was a "chump" behind his back, they would not say it to his face. He proved time and again that he was not weak because he was nice. He reminded me a little of my brother George. Good looking, but acted like he didn't know it.

I cannot imagine what could have gone wrong in his marriage, what woman in her right mind would throw a man like that away (present company excluded)!

But for sure life has taught me that there are always three sides to every story, **his, hers and the truth!**

Ralph was very smart like his dad; a dedicated worker, along with having excellent business ideas. He would be an asset to the company.

Since he was also going to be the liaison between the company and the clients, we had to work closely together. This gave us the opportunity to get reacquainted as adults, because until now, I had not seen him, but from a distance since he graduated and went away to school.

I was happy that we had always been friends, but was not sure how I felt about him coming back to Madisonville to work in our business. Not because I did not respect his work, but I didn't trust myself around him.

You see, I had a light crush on him in high school, but he never even looked in my direction. Miffed by that perceived slight, I went through my entire freshman year, believing that I hated him, **(*too slow to know I actually liked him*)**.

Being true to who I was at that time in my life, anger and alienation were the only ways I knew to deal with the emotions I did not understand. As a teenager being rejected by my mother was all the rejections I could take!

Now that he was back in my world, something about him made it difficult to be around him, *(still out of touch with my emotions).* Although I fought and denied it, I feared those old feelings coming back; needless to say, these feelings complicated things for me!

Diane said, this was good, that I was finally thawing out after Raymond. She thought my self-imposed man-fast was ridiculous. I wasn't being fair to myself, although she had the same vow. Since the death of her husband, she had not been in a relationship in almost twenty years.

So how was this different? She said it was different because her husband was the love of her life, and they were happy when they were together. He was *taken* from her, they didn't separate voluntarily. She said *His* love will always be enough for her. Now her world was her children, and her family, this arrangement worked fine for her and she was happy. None of my sister's thought that I should be alone.

Janet said "Peaches, you are too passionate to be without love in your life! You have to experience passion with a man while you are still young enough to enjoy it, without it giving you a heart attack!"

As *she laughed uncontrollably at my expense!* She said that it wasn't natural; God didn't intend for us to live alone. "Diane should not worry about you being alone, because what you are feeling around Ralph was smitten. He is making her weak!" I said in genuine horror, "Lord, I hope not!*" Now they are both laughing uncontrollably,* sisters!

In spite of the teasing from my sisters, I was not ready for a man in my life. I was committed to keeping myself busy with work. I stayed long hours at night when Raymond Sr. had the baby and didn't come out of my office during the day unless it was for a meeting or something more that I couldn't miss.

Most days Ralph was out on job sites; so work kept us apart as much as it had thrown us together, *but damn, that man was fine!* Since things in the business were changing so quickly, and we did not want to be moved out of our own company; my family decided to form sort of a board of directors to govern the business affairs. The board was made up of my family members and Billy's. I was included and so were Diane, Janet's husband Damon, Billy and now his son Ralph.

It was more of a management steering committee than a board, but we wanted some type of check and balance system so that the King family would have input into how the business is being run. We would not just walk away from my family business; it was still an important part of our family stability.

We wanted an outsider that didn't work for the company directly to be a part of the board, so we could vote on issues without biases. Deacon Fry was elected; he was an old friend of both families. Our office secretary was the board secretary as well-she would take notes at the meetings then send out copies of the minutes to each of us, and ensure that we completed the task listed during the meetings, via a task list.

The secretary, along with Billy's daughter would make sure that whatever tools or materials needed were ordered and provided to complete any task or changes that came up during meetings. I am sure that corporate American might consider it a crude system, but it worked for us. The Deacon was paid in bonuses donated to the church if the business showed a profit for the years he was acting as a board member.

We were not sure how official this all was, but the system succeeded in what we wanted to do; make my family feel that we were still an active part of my grandfather's company, and not be moved out without realizing it, because we were not hands on in the business.

Now, I know what you are thinking about Ralph; nice guy, smart, sweet, single, handsome in a wholesome big Bubba kind a way, working together almost every day. Why not test the water! Although time had passed since Vanessa's murder and Nea's, I was still a bit gun shy about men.

I am sure that I had only been on two dates in three years. I just could not work up the courage to make that move. I was too afraid of the unknown. There had been nothing going on in my world to convince me that I was wrong to run from relationships.

I needed guarantees and there were none. I didn't want to take a chance and make a wrong choice that would affect my family or my child. I just couldn't. How do you know when a man is going to be right for you?

I was so busy looking for crazy in a man's eyes; I could not see what else might be there.

Ralph *was* different, he seemed patient. I knew that he came from a good home. I had seen Billy with his wife and family for years. Billy has respect for his family and loved his wife; after all of these years they were still happy together.

They still laughed together, and he would send her flowers to the office some days just because, or show up unexpectedly to take her to lunch! I wondered what it might feel like to be loved like that.

To feel protected by the man in your life, and not afraid of saying or doing something that may cause him to laugh at you. Or living in constant fear of the next difference of opinion that would lead to a fight!

Ralph knew what my family had gone through over the past years and he knew about my relationship with Raymond and what happened between us, (*small town, and no secrets*).

He said that he would be honored to be my friend. Without me saying anything to him, he knew instinctively how I was feeling. He knew I was afraid of anything more.

As I grew more comfortable around him, I stopped running from interacting with him as a friend and coworker. I did not avoid him anymore, and when I was not acting like a love struck teenager, we worked well together.

Although I behaved better around him, and I did not run anymore, I did not seek him out either. Besides, I didn't need to hide, I had more self-control than that, I was not looking for a relationship and wasn't going to let **this burning need inside me every time I laid eyes on this man convince me otherwise!**

My sisters were enjoying my discomfort entirely too much. They even had my mother making fun of my fear at one of the family Sunday dinners!
Everyone knew Ralph was a good guy, and a good man, but aren't they all good in the beginning?

I was simply suffering from a very bad case of lust.
It had been almost four years since my divorce, I was only human you know! But I never, not one time, felt lust for my husband; perhaps I was going through some type of medical condition! ***"That was it, I needed to go and see a doctor!"*** Diane said, *"All you need is a strong man for a good hour-or two!"* ***(More uncontrollable laughter)!***

Sometimes Ralph and I went to lunch together and even dinner, under the guise of a "working lunch" or a "business dinner", as I said, when I wasn't being stupid we worked well together. We had similar ideas about ways of expanding the company, and we both wanted to take King's Decorating into the modern age. We even talked about a second office in Atlanta, with A.J., at the helm.

Billy would say that we would replace him and Ella in no time. He was still retired, but came in from time to time to consult on an expansion project or a big contract. But the difference between him and Ella and me and Ralph was that we were not a couple, we were just friends!

There was no denying that Ralph stirred something in me that I could not identify. He was so easy to talk to, we would talk for hours about anything and everything, and not realize how late it was getting, or how much time had passed.

I had heard about this type of man, but had never actually seen one. You know, like Angles-you believe they existed, but would you recognize one if you actually saw one up close?

My sister's started to tease me more and more about him- still I was not trying to make this into anything but what it was a friendship! After about six months of being friends, I invited Ralph to Sunday family dinner at Big Momma and Papa's house. Yes, we still had the tradition of Sunday Dinner at our family home.

We needed to hold on to something from our past--a time when we were all here, and happy together.

Ralph seemed to fit in quite nicely with the other men. They talked easily together, likely because they knew him as a boy, but we were still only friends, we had not kissed or even held hands. In spite of the lack of actual romance in our relationship, we spent most Sunday evenings together.

On Saturdays, we went to the park with my son; he was so good with him. I could see that it was not an act; he was sincere in his interest in him.

He came to my house for dinner several times over the next few months--sometimes I would cook and sometimes he would. It was a comfortable time that we spent together.

He would fix things around my house, like plumbing and build shelves for my townhouse garage--yes, it was comfortable. But as good as it was and as natural as it felt, I was still not sure that I could take it further.

Ralph did not push for more, he said he had respect for what I wanted and what I needed right now. He seemed to understand why I felt that way.

He did not make me feel like I was broken because I was affected by my painful past, and I was still trying to sort things out about the way I felt about relationships. I never had a relationship with a man where there was no pressure to do *something*, or make some choice, or respond to a request of some kind; A relationship where I did not need to perform, I did not recognize the feeling; **it was peace!**

After a year he asked that I go on an *official date* with him, he said that he wanted to spend time with me and that he has loved me since grammar school. But he knew that he didn't have a chance against Raymond, so he loved me from a distance. He asked me to not be afraid, but to allow him to love me and take care of me.

My reaction was to almost faint. Those words and the way he was looking at me almost made me scream and run away. It wasn't frightening, but it was scary. Remember, I was someone who did not know how to love or be loved. I didn't know where to begin!

This was exhausting. Couldn't we just continue things the way they were? Why did anything need to change? I apologized; I told him that I didn't know how to be happy in a relationship. I didn't know where to begin and that I did not know if I could do it. I was sorry, but I was not ready.

He said "fine I will not push you I have waited this long and I can wait longer. I am not going anywhere. I will just be here for you, whatever you need me to be."

Oh my Lord! "What was I going to do now?" I didn't know what to do or where to turn. If you think it was easy to come to work after that you are wrong!

I managed to look busy when he was around to avoid any conversation, but hello and good-bye, *(back to hiding my feelings)*. I know most men would say that I was messed up. I was broken, and that was correct, I was broken and I did not know if I could be fixed.

All of the relationships from my past only succeeded in making me feel incomplete. I did not trust my judgment regarding men and how to go about choosing the right man for me. Because of the lack of recourses of a nurturing female in my life, I had no one to talk to.

Big Momma was gone, and my sisters all thought I was crazy to not just go for it. Nevertheless, I wanted help with this, I had to speak with someone about how I was feeling to help me make a decision, and I needed advice.

Since Vanessa's passing my mother and I seemed to be able to interact without one of us making an excuse to leave the room because of the lack of an actual relationship. Now things were better between us. So, I took a chance--I went to my mother and presented my problem to her.

I tried to be honest about my feelings, as much as I could express them and she did listen. She was quieter for a second longer than I thought she should be if she was taking me seriously. I was beginning to feel that this was a mistake. She could never actually be sympathetic about me and what I might be going through. But when she finally spoke, she said, "Baby girl, you have had a hard time, we all have, but it is time to move on. Life is not going to stand still and wait.

If you don't move with it, you will be left behind. Fear is a natural reaction to pain and you have had so much, you don't want to be hurt again. You know what it feels like and of course no one wants to feel fear.

You know in your heart that Ralph is a good man, but you don't trust yourself to make the right decision. If I thought anything about him other than he is a good man for you, I would tell you. In spite of all that nonsense, I said to you about Raymond, I do know the difference. I know that you are afraid of making another mistake. You are afraid, if you are wrong, what's going to happen to you. How will it affect your son if you are wrong?"

"If you want love in your life take a chance on this man, but if you are really happy with your life the way it is, walk away. Know that you don't need to be in a relationship to be happy and have a full life. You have your son, your work, your family, so if that is enough for you, walk away. But don't turn him away because of fear."

"I apologize to you for all that I have done to feed that inner pain of yours. But it is time to let go of the pain baby, I cannot go back and change the past, but I can change today and today I want you to know that you deserve to be happy. Take a chance on love, go-and be happy!" I was shocked by what I just heard. Not at all what I expected to hear from *my Mother*!

I was still stuck on the apology, I think I missed most everything else she said to me that day, well not everything, I received the message -I deserved to be happy, but could Ralph make me happy? Could I make him happy? Is it even possible for another person to complete you?

There was only one way to find out. I told him that I was willing to try, but I was still not sure of myself. He would need to help me along. He would need to teach me about love, giving and receiving it, because I didn't know how.

He smiled and kissed me for the first time and I felt something warm inside me that went all the way to my toes-- I had never had that feeling with Raymond, *my sister Janet said it was passion, imagine that!*

"I WANT TO BE YOUR LAST LOVE"

Ralph was true to his word. He was patient and understanding and he allowed me time to ease into this new way of feeling. By no means was our relationship perfect, but nothing is. I didn't need it to be perfect; I needed it to be the truth! We disagreed of course sometimes. However, it was the way we disagree, that helped me to understand a healthy difference of opinion.

Two years later we were married Ralph and me. He treated my son like his own child; I hadn't expected that. It was an added bonus. We built a beautiful new house in the part of Madisonville that was once "white only," now black and white families are living easily side by side.

Our home is a brick two-story house. Kings Decorating built most of the cabinets, put in the floors and painted the walls, much of the work done by Ralph himself on the weekends. For the first time in my life, I was completely at peace. I still missed my sister and my cousin, but I believe that they are at peace now also.

It will never be okay that they were gone and the way they were taken from us still hurts me, but I think about them now and can talk about the fun we had. I can remember them and smile, no more fear of the same thing happening to me.

I remember them, knowing how blessed I was to have them in my life, even if it was for only a little while.

In spite of all I had been through, all that we lost, I found that life can be worth living, and that good things do come to those who wait! Before this, I would never believe I could be happy in a relationship, not just happy but comfortable, safe.

I am living proof that a victim of relationship violence, can heal from the abuse; move forward, and have a healthy relationship with a man.

Once I learned to love myself—when I realized that I deserved better and was determined not to settle for less than what I deserved, it found me and I was not even looking for it! Imagine that, **Big Momma didn't tell me this could happen!** I am in a relationship with a man that I love, and who loves me. I never imagined that I would feel secure in a situation that involved a man, other than the men in my family.

Being together forever feels like an adventure now, instead of a death sentence. If it can happen for me it can happen to other women, but ladies, we have to learn to love ourselves first. Honestly love yourself, before you can even hope to genuinely love someone else.

Believe that we deserve nothing but the best; respect, honesty and equal partnership in the relationship.

And even if he has all of the outside trappings the world tries to tell us we need to be happy with a man, you know what I am talking about; Money, power, good looks, position- but he dictates to you about who you are in the relationship, as if you or your opinion or contribution to the relationship is not important, that you don't matter.

Know that it will not change; he will not suddenly start to treat you like an equal- a partner and friend as well as a lover.

I am sure that some of you might think that I am tripping, *that women have to mold a man into the man you need him to be.*

But that, ladies is the problem. Some women want to believe when they meet a man with potential, you need to start *fixing him* so that he will see how valuable you are to him, and that now that he has you he cannot live without you!

Yes, it is important to bring something into the relationship -and yes, we can surely learn from each other, (you and your mate), and you should expect that type of exchange in relationships. But know that you cannot change someone or make him or her into who or what you want him or her to be. You can only change you! If you try to fix someone else, you are going to be disappointed.

If you believe that you can change a man by simply trying to be what you *think* he wants you to be, it's *you is tripping*. If this man does not value you and who you are from hello-- likely you are about to embark on a ride on the crazy train, drama not love.

He may not be abusive, verbally, physically or mentally, but he still may not be the man for you.
Know who you are first so that you will know the difference in what is for you, and want will not work for you.

Establish your boundaries for what you need to be okay, not only in a relationship but in your life. That way, when someone tries to cross those boundaries and you correct him, how he responds will give you a hint about what this man really wants from you. Does he want a partner in you, or someone he can control and manipulate? That is the question.

Ladies, a good relationship can happen if you pay attention to the warning signs and do not make excuses for his bad behavior; believe you deserve respect and consecration.

There are good men in the world- **no, all the good men are not married, dead or dating your uncle**, they are around! But you must know who you are in order to understand who the right man is for you; don't sell yourself short, you deserve to be happy! CLAIM it, OWN it and NEVER settle for less!

READERS' POLL

Dear readers,

Thank you for responding to my poll request to help me to finish my story. As I was writing about Peaches and her life, I predicted that we all would want her to have a happy ending, and that she deserved to find true love.

Although in *real* life is not always that way, the lesson here is, that there are good men in the world, and for everyone who wants love in their life, they can find it. But is there an alternative? Can there be a happy ending different than the man of your dreams showing up and the two of you living *happily ever after?* What does that mean for the rest of the women in the world, trying to live life on their own? No Prince in sight!

So I decided to include both endings rather than choosing one! Different, I am sure, but because your response to each ending was so evenly divided, and since this book is my first fiction work; I want to give all of my readers what they wanted! So read on, and I hope you enjoy the second ending!

I would love to hear from you, visit our blog or go to the website and leave a comment!

www.inamaegreene.org

Also look for my new book, A.J.'s story, *"**Men Cry at Night**"* available Fall, 2016. Find out what happens to A.J. after he moved away from Madisonville to Atlanta, Georgia, in the hope of finding peace after the tragic death of his sister Nea, and resolution after a painful and messy divorce from his wife Tina. Relationship violence can affect men also; see how A.J. finds love and fulfillment after an abusive marriage, in this continuing saga of the King Family!

ALTERNATIVE ENDING
"IF DREAMS REALLY DO COME TRUE"

I would love all women in the world to have this same type of happy ending that Ralph and I had.
I know as you were reading my story, you all wanted it to come out all right for Peaches; like it always does in made up stories about life. But in real life, too often the ending is not so happy. Not necessarily tragic, but not story book either. This is real life, and in real life, you cannot write yourself a happy ending.

What if my real ending was not so perfect? What should you do when the ending doesn't turn out quite like you want, what can you do? How do you move on? Let us look at my story and what would happen if Ralph and I did not get married. What if I decided to just keep it simple, only continuing to date?

Would that be okay? Could you live with it? Let us pretend that things were different for Peaches and her ending looks and sound a bit like this alternative ending.

Why burst your bubble, when you can bask in the typical storybook tale of love and life? Because this is a lesson, I want you to be prepared to deal with **life for real**, and things do not always go the way you want. How do we learn to live with disappointments? Humor me, and let's look at a different ending to my story!

"Will You Still Love Me Tomorrow"?!

Ralph and I are friends, and we will remain close friends to this day; but no marriage, no house and picket fence, and no happily ever after, not in the traditional way.
The truth is, after talking with my mother, I realized that:
1.) My life was fine the way it was and,
2.) Marriage was not something I was looking for right now.

Yes, I enjoyed his company, and yes, he is a good man, but in all honesty, I did not want him as a husband.

This time I listened to myself, and I accepted **what I wanted out of life.** Someday that might change, but today I did not want marriage. Does that make me slow or stupid? Or a woman who knows her own mind and is not afraid to do what I want, and not what is expected of me!

My sister Diane said that I was brave to want to go it alone. Not brave, just wanting to live *my life on my own terms!* If the meaning of being true to yourself includes doing what you want with your life, then I am simply being true to myself.

I made the mistake of doing what I thought everyone else wanted me to do with my life before, and it turned out horribly, almost tragically. This is my life to live and I am going to learn from my mistakes and live how I want, based on what I have learned is right for me! Is it selfish to want to be on my own? Not at all! That is a guilt trip that society has placed on young women so that we would not be resistant to following the rules.

There **was** a reason why I was taking my time with this relationship, in spite of what my family and my friends were advising me to do. My instincts were screaming the truth at me all along. This is the reason it had taken me so long to agree to go out on an actual date with him, (YOU THINK)!

When I married Raymond we both chose to ignore our instincts; that voice in our head, speaking to us through the cheating, the lack of common interest, and lack of respect, all telling us that we were not a good match.

My spirit knew, even if I didn't that our marriage was not **my** dream for me. It was everyone else's wish for my life. Although a lovely one, it was not necessary for me to feel complete. Unlike with Raymond, I am no longer trying to convince myself that marriage *was the natural next step* **in** my life! Big Momma never said that I could be happy on my own; that I could love my family and friends that I care about and I can have a complete life, without being someone's *wife.*

In fairness to Big Momma, in her day it was unheard of for a woman of marriageable age to be single. In her time, your purpose as a woman was to marry and raise a family.

Don't get me wrong, it is okay to want a mate and partner, but first I need it be true to me. Before I can love someone else, I had to learn to love myself.

Ladies, what will we give up, give away, throw away, change about who we are, **to have a man?**

Too many of us don't take the time to understand what we need to be happy. I suppose it is too much work when you are on a mission to be married to the man of your dreams and pregnant with your second child by age thirty!

So if he looks good and is employed, and he doesn't have a criminal record (that you know of), he is a good catch! If we don't understand what we will and will not allow in a relationship (setting boundaries), how can we know what will truly make us happy? How do we know who is the right mate for us? How can we choose?

Or do we skip over that step because we are afraid that we will never meet a man that can fulfill **all** of our needs. And if we ask too much of him, he might flee, he's only human right? Besides, our new man might not agree with the limits we set, and then what will we do? FIND A MAN WHO WILL!

Don't believe me? See how you do on this test; (be honest)!

1. What has the man you JUST met done for you that will cause you to have sex with him after only a couple of dates?
2. If the man you JUST met said that he likes women with long hair, how likely are you to get a hair weave?
3. If you are a NOT athletic and the man you JUST met plays tennis or golf, how likely are you to take up one of these sports, although it has never been anything you ever wanted to do?
4. You meet a man in a bar or at a party and tell him your life story (as we often do), and when he says "I would never treat you that way, I know how to treat a good woman," and **you believe him?!**
5. Your new boyfriend (of a few months) does not like your friends and tells you not to hang out with them anymore, you: a.) Tell him where to jump b.) Tell your girls, you can't hang out with them anymore c.) Lie to him and tell him you don't see them, but try and work them in when you can?

I could go on, but I think you get where I am coming from!

I learned a lot about myself during the past few years. I found that there are good men in this world; my uncles are good fathers and husbands, my brother and brother in law-also good fathers and husbands.

I would never say they are perfect, but no one is. What made them different; there are no signs of the tragic legacy that has followed our family for decades-no wife beating, and no disrespect to the women in their lives, (confirmation that to abuse is a choice).

What happened to Aunt Bee, Vanessa and Nea were horrible tragedies. The truth is, yes, some behavior in families is learned behavior, not a curse. That is why we need to talk openly to our children about relationships and how to interact with someone of the opposite sex, in a healthy way, with real and attainable relationship expatiations.

Ladies, here is the deal; life is what you make of it! You cannot spend your life waiting and looking for Mr. Right, because he might not show up, then where will you be.

So what if all of your friends are married, what has that to do with **your** life? Watching and looking for something or someone to complete you who might not show, is a tragic waste of your life. However, here is the good news; you can make it on your own.

Yes, there is life after divorce, and after break up, bad or other. Often women (me included) run out of one relationship right into another. It is never going to be healthy ***to end one relationship and then jump on the next man you see and try to ride him into a happy ending.*** Before you start a new relationship, give yourself time to heal, and time to reflect on what went wrong with the last relationship; was it you or him? *(Yes girls, there are times when we are to blame for the breakup)!*

I am telling you this because likely no one else has. In order to be happy with your life, you have to **know you**. Take off the blindfolds and look at yourself, and accept what you see. Learn that you can be a complete person, on your own, that you can be happy and not be part of a couple.

Ladies, you should not put the pressure on yourself to have it all, if that includes a husband, picket fence and 2.5 children, when deep down it might not be what you really want. I know now that I do not need a married relationship to feel whole. Of course we all want that special someone in our lives to spend time with (I do have that in Ralph), but the way the relationship is now- is how I choose to have him in my life. (Doing what is right for me)!

Do what is right for **you** ladies, not what your grandmother says you need, what your best friend or the latest reality show say you need, but what **you** *know you need based on understanding yourself!*

Having a life plan that puts you first does not necessarily consist of *a list of the 10 things every woman should do to catch a man!* I am not done with learning about life. I need more time to get to know me.

HOWEVER, if he does not show up, I am not going to feel like I failed or that life had dealt me a bad hand or that there is something wrong with **me** because I do not have a man. This is not male bashing; this is me loving me first!
Find yourself first ladies.

Know who you are, with and without a mate-so that a good relationship will be one of the *many* things in your life that brings you joy, and not cause you to sacrifice who you are.

We are so much more than a plus one. This is the lessons that you should be sharing with your children.

Do not take on a bad relationship simply because it is a relationship, and then decide to make it enough, when you know that it is not enough for you, but it is easier than waiting for what you really want and deserve.

I am happier than I have ever been. I have a male friend who I trust in my life. We are two consenting adults and I trust him to tell me the truth, to respect my opinions and choices, and not make me pay for them later when they don't agree with his. *Yes, ladies, I am giving you permission, live your life on your terms!*

If you think my family is not tripping you are wrong. I love my family, but they have their lives and I have mine, and I cannot live based on what they think I should do. I have to live on my terms, for my son and me!

I am helping you to accept the truth, to accept that because you are alone you are not necessarily lonely!

The world is not full of storybook happy endings, so don't expect it, or force it when it doesn't show up.

But know the ending can be happy, without the *story that tells us that we, each and every one of us, need a mate to be complete!* Surely not at any cost (verbal abuse, physical abuse or abuse of any kind)!

Now if you do find Mr. Right (you go girl), that is a blessing, and I wish you well. But before you take the bait, insure that the relationship will be an addition to your life, and not a requirement! I am not saying to stop dreaming, it's ok to dream, I am saying to realize that the dream doesn't define you, and if it doesn't come true, you are still you, and you are relevant, that your life matters.

I know that there are some good men in the world, and some bad. I have proof that not all men are like my grandfather, or Raymond's father. And that I have a choice in all of this, unlike my grandmother, who had choices, but because of the time she lived in, she didn't realize it. She had the right to walk away from my grandfather and his bad behavior at any time, **but she** didn't know how!

What makes me sadder than anything is that today, with all the information about relationship violence available to us; women are still caught up in situations that cost them everything. (No one should **die** to be in love!)

With all of the resources available to help victims of domestic violence, we don't look for a way out, we believe *that we have to sleep in the bed we made,* and make the relationship work. It's not true, you can leave, it is okay to leave!

Please know, likely the right man for you is out there. But anything you do, any choices you make, make with you in mind, knowing that you deserve to be happy, feeling safe in your own home is a right, not a luxury, and no man is worth your life!

THE END
For real this time

AFTERWORD

November of 2014, I lost a friend to relationship violence, dating violence to be exact.
She was smart, she was beautiful, and she dated a man that by her own admission, she was afraid of, a man that she wanted to break up with but did not know how to do it.

I told her in details that I may not share with a lot of victims. Being an advocate for victims of abuse, I was not sure about how they would receive the information, but since this was my friend, I did extend past those boundaries. With my friend, I was personal. And I was intense and I was serious!

She asked that I step outside my role of advocate and just be her friend and to keep her secret, not to tell her family, she didn't want them to worry.

She said she would break it off with him, and do the things that I had suggested her to do. I gave her a list, a checklist on how to leave this man that she was afraid of. She said that she would follow it, starting today!

They were just dating; they were not married, not living together, this should have made it easier for her to get away from him. They did not have any children together, no business connections, just dating.

About a week after our conversation, I asked her how she was doing and how the breakup went, she began to show signs that she did not want to talk about this with me. I respected her request for space (although it was not a verbal request), for now. I have been a victim's advocate for nine years, working with victims and their families, doing workshops and seminars regarding awareness topics. I recognized the body language. I waited another week and asked my friend that question again. Again, she put me off.

My fear was that my friend was backsliding, that she either was reconsidering the break up or had already taken him back. Like most victims, she was ashamed to tell me or anyone that she had changed her mind about him, (if that is what it was), or that she had not broken up with him at all because she didn't think it was necessary, they were better, that he was sorry. I spoke with her again, this time even though I know she was not trying to hear me.

I asked her to not underestimate him. I realize that most women think that they know the men they are dating, or married to after all he has been an intimate part of their life for years, months, sometimes only for a few weeks!

After all, they have seen each other in the most personal and intimate of situations. Some women are married to these men; they have children with these men, they are the first boyfriends they ever had and so on.

Many women feel that they know the men in their lives so well that they can predict their behavior, what they will and will not do, how far they will go when angry and what boundaries they will cross, or not!

Sadly, too many women are wrong about the men in their lives. An article in the Huffington Post "30 shocking domestic violence statics", says that "roughly 4,774,000 women experience physical violence by an intimate partner each year and that since 2003, 18,000 women in this country were murder victims of intimate partners".

However, since often-family violence or relationship violence goes unreported, or because of lack of evidence, the crime can be ruled an accident or even as a suicide, so that number is likely much higher.

After our conversation, my friend went on her way-- going about her busy and full life as she usually did.

We spoke again a couple of times just before Thanksgiving. We promised to get together the first of the year, when we were both back to business as usual, regular life activities after the holiday, you know, normal!

However the Monday after Thanksgiving, just five days since I last saw her, spoke with her, hugged her and promised to talk soon. I was shocked to see my friends pretty face flash across my television screen in the wee hours of the morning on the morning news.

I was afraid to turn up the volume, afraid of what I might hear, of what I know they were saying about my friend.
My very worst fear had been realized; my friend was dead. She was the victim of a gunshot wound, found dead the weekend after Thanksgiving in her apartment, by her family.

How did this happen to my friend and countless other women in this country?

My friend like many women did not believe he would go that far. Oh yes, he would threaten, and yell and maybe even throw things, but he would never go that far! -Not so far as to actually hurt her, no he wouldn't, after all these things only happen to other women, other people, other families-not to you or people you know!

Although this book is a work of fiction, and the people, places and events are made up, a figment of my imagination, the story about my friend is true.

Sadly, in the same way that I am telling this story in my book about a family in the south who suffered too much because of this crime, although they are made up by me, it is the true story of too many lives destroyed by relationship violence in this country.

My heart is broken by this crime again, devastated *again* by this crime that has claimed the life of my aunt (my mother's sister), my own sister and my cousin. The wind has been knocked out of me *again*. In the same way it has all of the other times before. But I will not allow it to slow me down. There should be a mandatory policy in all counties that requires all police agencies to contact the victim when the perpetrator is being released.

Laws that require government monies are provided to properly fund shelters and other victim service agencies, so the women affected by this crime can get the help she needs to save her life. America, we must establish programs and campaigns that will remove the stigma associated with relationship violence. A stigma that may cause a victim to feel shame because she is being affected by this crime and this shame might prevent her from getting the help she so desperately needs.

If you or someone you know is a victim of relationship violence there is help for you, please call the National Domestic Violence Hotline number –1800-799 SAFE (7233) for help information in your area.

Also, there is a section of resources in the back of this book where you can go to get help, safely and confidently. Please, enjoy the book, and receive the message-- domestic violence kills, get out, get help, you deserve better you deserve to live!

Darlene Greene-Barree
Author

WHERE TO GO FOR HELP

DOMESTIC VIOLENCE RESOURCE HELP
DOMESTIC VIOLENCE HELP LINE NUMBER 1800-799-7233

The human race has evolved beyond the age where women are property, we are more than a commodity, yet sadly, one in every four women will experience domestic violence in her lifetime.

In 70-80% of intimate partner homicides, no matter, which partner was killed; the man physically abused the woman before the murder.

Domestic violence is against the law and yet more than 5,000,000 women a year are victimized by relationship violence in the United States in some form; domestic violence, dating violence, sexual assault, LGBT batter to name a few.

This crime knows no boundaries, it has no respect for race or religion, and no social economic group is immune to relationship violence and its devastating effects on the victim and his/her family, it can happen to anyone.

A woman will need to know more than to recognize the warning signs that someone you meet could become abusive toward you or someone you love. A victim of abuse needs to know how to leave a violent relationship safely; she will need to develop a safety plan.

A safety plan is a blueprint for your safety that will give you some direction on how to leave your abuser safely.

It can also direct a victim and her family to other services, counseling help, shelter, and other victim's services that can help anyone who finds that they are in a violent and abusive relationship.

The important thing to know is that you can get help. On the following pages we have compiled a list of different victim's services across the country, If you cannot find the service that you need among our list of resources, please call the National Domestic Hotline number 1-800-799- (SAFE) 7233, they will help you to locate victims' services in your area.

RED FLAGS AND WARNING SIGNS

From my book: When You Live In Fear-How To Get Out Of A Relationship That Is Killing You!

On my radio show and in my lectures we talk about the Red Flags and Warning Signs in relationships that could lead to violence.

Things that women, both young and mature should pay attention to regarding the behavior of the person they are dating.

I suggest that if the men in their lives are doing three out of the twelve things listed--- maybe this is a relationship that you might want to reevaluate.

I have read these words hundreds of times over the years.

Giving information to women and teen's at my lectures and seminars, and in my books, and yet too often I can see that same woman or teen again and they will tell me that they should have listened. That they should have believed that the man in their life was capable of not only one, but perhaps several if the things in the list attached.

The safest thing that a person who is in an abusive relationship can do to save herself is to believe that if this man has a history of abuse or he exhibits violent or unhealthy behavior, do not second-guess your instincts. Leave before you are hurt or worse.

I say after each book that I do not need to list the Red Flags or the Safety Plan or the Resource list; we have them listed every place, books, pamphlets, our website, and yet women and men continue to fall victims to this crime.

My husband says that I should continue to include them and any other information that will help anyone who in an abusive situation until the women and men in our country know and began to understand what they are up against.
So here, they are again, the Red Flags and the list of How to Help a Friend, along with resources by state, and I will continue to print them and talk about them until this crime is no more!

I will continue to say the same thing over and over until we get it! Until our natural reaction to unhealthy behavior in a relationship is to run in the opposite direction, not give in to the benefit of the doubt—until violence in relationships is a thing of the past!

BECAUSE THE ROAD TO SAFETY SHOULD NOT BE A DEAD-END!

RED FLAGS

Heavy drinking or drug abuse: (especially if he uses substances as an excuse for what he does, "the alcohols made me do it.")

Abuse during the courtship period: is a guarantee of further abuse that will become more frequent and severe. Don't marry him with the belief that "I can change him." You won't.

Morbid jealousy: This may be a bit flattering at first, but will be a curse later on. You will never convince him that you are innocent of his accusations.

Past child abuse and/or witness of marital violence:
This happens in some cases. Children learn from what they see men often discipline their own children as they were taught. He may be a "violence carrier".

Inability to handle frustration: If he blows up and explodes at small things and reacts with a tantrum over minor things, he may act out frustration with violence in a marriage. How he deals with anger is the key.

A violent temper: This speaks for itself. If you feel fear when he acts out his anger, that fear is a warning signal. Listen to it!

Cruelty to animals, abuse and mistreatment of pets:
Great enjoyment of hunting for the sake of killing animals could help you to face this question: What makes you know he will treat you any differently?

Preoccupation with weapons: They are an extension of self. A person is what she/he lives. If he ever "playfully" points a gun at you or ever gestures at you with another weapon, what could happen if he became very angry with you?

Mental illness: A person with an unsound mind or without any sense of moral responsibility or guilt may not be in control of his actions. Does he act in ways that you feel are abnormal or strange?

A poor self-image, insecurity about his own masculinity: If he feels compulsive about always being dominating one lives out a macho role at all times, you will be subject to his control and possibly treated like one of his possessions. He may feel he has the right to treat you like his property to do as he pleases.

A pattern of blaming others: Particularly, his wife for his problems: If he never accepts his faults and responsibilities when things go wrong, be ready to be blamed for everything.

Acceptance of violence: As an appropriate problem solving method. Do you want a man who talks out or acts out his anger?

LEGAL HELP, CHILD CUSTODY AND DIVORCE

The Domestic Violence Survival Kit (www.dvguide.com) is an invaluable resource in all matters to do with the police, protection orders and the law regarding domestic violence.

Call your local county court house and ask for "family law". Most courthouses now have a clerk who can help lay people understand the law and answer questions. Many now have web sites describing the procedures for filing divorce, protection orders and arranging child custody in your area.

Call your State Coalition on Domestic Violence for additional information in your state or go to www.feminist.org (Click Hotlines, Domestic Violence Resources).

You can always call the National Domestic Violence Hotline (1-800-799-7233) for information on the law in your state. Women's Divorce- Helping Women survive divorce and rebuild their lives http://www.womansdivorce.com/abusive-relationships.htmlhttp//www.Womenslaw.org ...because knowledge is power

HOW TO HELP A FRIEND WHO IS IN AN ABUSIVE RELATIONSHIP

Step 1
Say to her that you are concerned about her, her safety and the safety of her children. Tell her that she deserves better and you want to see her happy, that no one should be afraid in their home, not her and certainly not her children.

Step 2
Listen as your friend confides in you about her abuse. Let her know that you care about her and that you want to help, but do not try to make the decisions for her to leave. The choice has to be hers. Do not criticize her behavior or her abusive partner. We do not want her to shift her focus from getting help to defending his behavior.

Step 3
Be a part of your friend's safety plan. Encourage her to pack her most important belongings in a suitcase and leave it at your house so she is ready to leave whenever she has to. HelpGuide.org recommends she have clothing, money, important documents and emergency contacts in her safety kit.

Step 4
Do not withdraw your support if your friend makes a decision you do not like or decides to go back to her abuser. Abuse takes a toll mentally, physically and emotionally on women and she may make several attempts before she is able to leave. Her abuser also may be threatening her or her family, so she may decide to take some time and regroup or rethink her strategy. Support her during those times as well.

Step 5
Call the police immediately and send them to her house if you witness abuse, or if she calls you to tell you that her partner is currently abusing her. Do not hesitate and do not try to go to her house to break things up.
It is never a good idea to confront her abuser because he could harm you or take his anger out on her once you have left because you got involved.

MY CHECK LIST FOR LOVING ME FIRST

1. DO I WANT TO DATE OR DO I WANT A SERIOUS RELATIONSHIP? (Honest answer).
2. Am I dating because that is what I want or is pressure from family and friends causing me to look for a mate?
3. Do I REALLY like this guy/girl or am I making due because I will likely not meet anyone better?
4. When we are together, I feel happy and carefree, or am I always on edge trying not to do or say anything that will offend him/her?
5. Am I accepting excuses for his bad behavior because I like him/her and I want things to work out? Or do I believe that he is REALLY trying?
6. When I describe my boundaries and my non-negotiable, does he understand and support my choices, or does he try to change my mind, often getting angry because I will not bend to his will?
7. When I disagree with him, does he respect my opinion or does he argue with me and try to force me to agree with him?
8. Is it okay with him when I want to spend time away from him with an activity that does not include him, or does he pout and complain that I am always too busy?
9. Does he respect my privacy and does not try to look at my phone to see who I am calling and texting or not try to read my emails?
10. Is my relationship with my children, friends and other family members an issue for him, or does he respect and support the time I spend with them?

If you could not answer yes to eight out of ten of these questions, then maybe the relationship you are in or the reason for the relationship is not healthy and perhaps you should take another look at why you are with this person.

Resource List

www.domesticshelters.org
National Domestic Violence Hotline-800-799-SAFE- (7233)
National Coalition Against Domestic Violence-www.ncadv.org

Resources and help agencies by state

Arizona Coalition Against Domestic Violence
100 West Camelback Street, Suite 109
Phoenix, AZ 85013
Phone: 602-279-2900
FAX: 602-279-2980

Arkansas Coalition Against Domestic Violence
#1 Sheriff Lane, Suite C
North Little Rock, AR 72114
Phone: 501-812-0571
FAX: 501-812-0578

California Alliance Against Domestic Violence - Southern Office
8929 S. Sepulveda Blvd., Suite 520
Los Angeles CA 90045-3605
Telephone 310-649-2479
Fax 310-649-3953

Statewide California Coalition for Battered Women
3711 Long Beach Blvd., #718
Long Beach, CA 90807
Telephone: 562-981-1202
Fax: 562-981-3202
Toll-free: 888-722-2952
E-mail: sccbw@sccbw.org

Colorado Coalition Against Domestic Violence
P.O. Box 18902
Denver, CO 80218
Phone: 303-831-9632
FAX: 303-832-7067

Connecticut Coalition Against Domestic Violence
106 Pitken Street
East Hartford, CT 06108
860-282-7899
FAX: 860-282-7892
800-281-1481 (In State)
888-774-2900 (In State Hotline)

DC Coalition Against Domestic Violence
513 U Street, NW
Washington, DC 20001
202-387-5630 (phone)
202-387-5684 (fax)
dccadv@aol.com (email)

Florida Coalition Against Domestic Violence
308 E. Park Avenue
Tallahassee, FL 32301
(850) 425-2749
Fax: (850) 425-3091
TDD: (850) 621-4202
In-state: 800-500-1119

Georgia Coalition on Family Violence
1827 Powers Ferry Road, Bldgs. 3, Suite 325
Atlanta, GA 30339
Phone: 770-984-0085
FAX: 770-984-0068
800-334-2836 (In State Hotline)

Prevent Child Abuse Georgia
1720 Peachtree Street NW, Suite 600
Atlanta, Georgia 30309
1-800-CHILDREN

Hawaii State Coalition Against Domestic Violence
98-939 Moanalua Road
Aiea, HI 96701-5012
Phone: 808-486-5072
FAX: 808-486-5169

Idaho Coalition Against Sexual and Domestic Violence
815 Park Blvd., Suite 140
Boise, ID 83712
Phone: 208-384-0419
FAX: 208-331-0687
E-mail: domvio@micron.net

Illinois Coalition Against Domestic Violence
801 S. 11th St.
Springfield, IL 62703
Phone: 217-789-2830
FAX: 217-789-1939

Indiana Coalition Against Domestic Violence
2511 E. 46th Street, Suite N-3

Indianapolis, IN 46205
TOLL-FREE: 800-332-7385
Phone: 317-543-3908
FAX: 317-377-7050

Iowa Coalition Against Domestic Violence
2603 Bell Avenue, Suite 100
Des Moines, IA 50321
Phone: 515-244-8028
FAX: 515-244-7417
In-State Hotline (Not part of the Coalition) 800-942-0333

Kansas Coalition Against Sexual and Domestic Violence
220 SW 33rd Street, Suite 100
Topeka, KS 66611
Phone: 785-232-9784
FAX: 785-266-1874

Kentucky Domestic Violence Association
P.O. Box 356
Frankfort, KY 40602
Phone: 502-695-2444
FAX: 502-695-2488
Victim Impact Statement
Sexual Assault Connection

Louisiana Coalition Against Domestic Violence
P.O. Box 77308
Baton Rouge, Los Angeles 70879
Phone: 225-752-1296
FAX: 222-751-8927

Maine Coalition to End Domestic Violence

128 Main Street
Bangor, ME 04401
Phone: 207-941-1194
FAX: 207-941-2327

Maryland Network Against Domestic Violence
6911 Laurel Bowie Road, Suite 309
Bowie, MD 20715
TOLL-FREE: 800-MD-HELPS
Phone: 301-352-4574
FAX: 301-809-0422

Massachusetts Coalition Against Sexual Assault and Domestic Violence
Jane Doe, Inc.
14 Beacon Street, Suite 507
Boston, MA 02108
Phone: 617-248-0922
FAX: 617-248-0902

Michigan Coalition Against Domestic & Sexual Violence
3893 Okemos Road, Ste B2
Okemos MI 48864
ph.: 517-347-7000
fax: 517-347-1377

Minnesota Coalition for Battered Women
450 North Syndicate Street, Suite 122
St. Paul, MN 55104
Phone: 612-646-6177
FAX: 612-646-1527
(800) 289-6177

Mississippi State Coalition Against Domestic Violence
P.O. Box 4703
Jackson, MS 39296-4703
TOLL-FREE: 800-898-3234
Phone: 601-981-9196
FAX: 601-981-2501
Protection Order

Missouri Coalition Against Domestic Violence
415 East McCarty
Jefferson City, MO 65101
Phone: 573-634-4161
FAX: 573-636-3728

Domestic Violence Connection
Montana Coalition Against Domestic and Sexual Violence
Child Advocacy Project
PO Box 633
Helena, MT 59624
406.443.7794 phone
406.443.7818 fax

carmenhotvedt@care2.com
Nebraska Domestic Violence and Sexual Assault Coalition
825 M Street, Suite 404
Lincoln, NE 68508-2253
In-State Toll Free: 800-876-6238
Phone: 402-476-6256
FAX: 402-476-6806

SAFETY PLAN WORKBOOK

Personal Safety Plan Workbook

Often, if you write something out it is easier to remember, this workbook will assist you in thinking through some issues that will be important if you are planning to leave your abuser.

Step 1: Safety during a violent incident

Women cannot always avoid violent incidents. In order to increase safety, battered women may use a variety of strategies. This is just a few of the things that you might think about to help you stay safe in a violent situation: Your shelter will be happy to help you with your safety plan if you are not sure how to begin.

A. If I decide to leave, I will

_____
_____
_____
_____

_____

(Practice how to get out safely. What doors, windows, elevators, stairwells or fire escapes will you use?)

B. I can keep my purse and car keys ready and put them _____ (list place) in order to leave quickly.

C. I can tell _____ and
_____ about the violence and request they call the police if they hear suspicious noises coming from my house.

D. I can teach my children how to use the telephone to contact the police and fire department.

E. I will use _____ as my code for my children or my friends so they can call for help.

F. If I have to leave my home, I will go
_____

G. I can also teach some of these strategies to some or all of my Children. When I expect we are going to have an argument, I will try to move to a space that is lowest risk, such as
_____

(Try to avoid arguments in the bathroom, garage, and kitchen, near weapons or in rooms without access to an outside door).

I will use my judgment and intuition. If the situation is very serious, I can give my partner what he/she wants to calm him/her down. I have to protect myself until we are out of danger.

Step 2: Safety when preparing to leave

Battered women frequently leave the residence they share with the battering partner. Leaving must be done with a careful plan in order to increase safety. Batterers often strike back when they believe that a battered woman is leaving the relationship.

I can use some or all of the following safety strategies:

A. I will leave money and an extra set of keys with _____ so that I can leave quickly.

B. I will keep copies of important documents or keys at _____

C. I will open a saving account by _____ to increase my independence.

D. Other things I can do to increase my independence include
_____
_____
_____
_____
_____.

E. The domestic violence hotline number in my city is
_____.

The National Domestic Violence Hotline number is 1-800-799-SAFE. I can seek shelter by calling this number.

F. I can purchase a pre-paid phone and keep it with me at all times.
I understand that if I use my telephone at home or our family cell phone, the following month the telephone bill will tell my batterer those numbers I called after I left.
To keep my telephone communications confidential, either I must use my prepaid cell phone or I might get a friend to add me to her cell phone plan for a limited time when I first leave.

G. I will check with _____ and _____ to see who would be able to let me stay with them or lend me some money.

H. I can leave extra clothes with _____

I. I will sit down and review my safety plan every_____ in order to plan the safest way to leave the residence. My friend or domestic violence advocate _____ has agreed to help me review this plan.

J. I will rehearse my escape plan and, as appropriate, practice it with my children.

Step 3: Safety in my own home

There are many things a woman can do to increase her safety in her own residence. It may be impossible to do everything at once, but safety measures can be added step-by-step. Safety measures to use should include:

I can change the locks on my doors and windows as soon as possible. I can replace wooden doors with steel/metal doors.

I can install security systems, including additional locks, window bars, poles to wedge against doors, and electronic system, etc.

I can purchase rope ladders to be used for escape from second-story windows.

I can install smoke detectors and protectors and purchase fire extinguishers for each floor in my house or apartment.

I can install an outside lighting system that lights up when a person is coming close to the house.

I will teach my children how to use the telephone to make a collect call to me and to

_____

(friend/minister/other) in the event my partner takes the children.

I will tell people who take care of my children which people have permission to pick up my children and that my partner is not permitted to do so. The people I will inform about pick-up permission include:

_____

School

_____

Daycare

_____

Babysitter

_____

Sunday School Teacher

_____

Teacher

Others
I can inform the following people that my partner no longer resides with me and they should call the police if he is observed near my home.

_____

Neighbors

_____

Pastor

_____

Friends

References

When You Live In Fear How to Get Out of A Relationship that is Killing you (DGreene 2001)

Jim Crow Laws. http://www.sju.edu/~brokes/jimcrow.htm. (1/24/02)

http://www.oprah.com/index.html(2015)

Huffington Post "30 shocking domestic violence statistics http://www.huffingtonpost.com/2014/10/23/domestic-violence-statistics_n_5959776.html

Girlhood in America: A-G--edited by Miriam Forman-Brunell

AUTHOR'S NOTES

There have been hundreds of books written about domestic violence in the past three decades. I chose that time frame, because over the past twenty years, there have been definite strides made in the battle against domestic violence, milestones that have caused our country to raise awareness, and provide resources and education, to support the victims of this crime and their families.

However, each year, thousands of women in the United States continue to die from the crime of relationship violence.

In spite of that fact, I know that by simply adding the words DOMESTIC VIOLENCE in the beginning of my book, some of you will not want to read it. Not because you don't like to read, but like most people you think that this crime will never happen to you or someone you care about; so there is no point in opening yourself up to a tragedy that will not affect you! OR, you are in an abusive relationship, and are not ready to face the reality, that this crime has happened to you and your family. You are not ready to face that if you don't make changes in your life today, it could end tragically.

Likely, you don't want to face the reality that the man you love, or are living with, or is the father of your children, could actually kill you or seriously injure you, or your child.

Of course, no one wants to face that--hear that--or be forced to look at the fact that, your life is in more danger in your own home than on the street. Who wants to look at that, or face this bleak and frightening reality, when you can continue to walk around in a cloud of denial hoping for the best?

Who wants to talk about making changes, when you can continue to pray that you really do know this man in your life, like you think you do? And, that he will never go so far as to actually hurt you. As long as you can tell yourself that this terrible thing will never happen to you, and, as long as you can continue to believe the lie that you are telling your family, and friends . . . the lie that you have told so many times over, and over the last few years or months, that you are now beginning to believe it yourself. Okay then, this book is not a book you are going to read. But for the rest of you, those of you who want to know how to leave, and how to live; how to survive your violent relationship, please read my story, and learn from my family history. If you only get as far as this page, take this information with you, that you have a choice, and that there is help, you can get out, and you can survive. But first, you need to ask for help, and you must make the choice to save your life.

ABOUT THE AUTHOR

As a native of Chicago, Darlene's life changed forever when her youngest sister Ina Mae was lost to domestic violence. This tragedy prompted her to develop an organization where women in crisis could go to receive help and resources to escape potentially deadly situations. The Ina Mae Greene Foundation-For My Sisters a 501c3 is an educational, resource and information foundation. The foundation's objective is to raise awareness about the atrocities of domestic abuse. Darlene is a very passionate speaker and lecturer on the topic of domestic violence and domestic abuse.

In addition to conducting dating violence awareness training and teen dating violence education, Ms. Greene lectures on how to leave an abusive relationship safely. She is the author of two important Domestic Violence safety and resource books; **"WHEN YOU LIVE IN FEAR: HOW TO GET OUT OF A RELATIONSHIP THAT IS KILLING YOU!"** This book is a resource and information guide for victims of domestic abuse who are trying to leave a dangerous relationship, and **BLOOD RELATIVES: BREAKING, THE CYCLE… BREAKING THE SILENCE (EXPOSING THE UGLINESS OF DOMESTIC VIOLENCE),** the true story of three women in Darlene's family who were murdered by men they dated .Darlene lives in Dallas Texas with her husband, son, two steps sons, and six grandchildren.